LIVE UNITED

United Way
of Portage County

www.uwportage.org

ROBODAD

RoboDad

Alden R. Carter

G. P. Putnam's Sons • New York

ACKNOWLEDGMENTS Many thanks to all who helped with *RoboDad,* particularly my editor, Refna Wilkin; my agent, Jonathon Lazear, and his staff; my mother, Hilda Carter Fletcher; and my friends Dean Markwardt and Judy Davis. I am especially indebted to Dr. Michel Roy for the many hours he spent on the manuscript. As always, my wife, Carol, deserves much of the credit.

Published by G. P. Putnam's Sons, a division of The Putnam & Grosset Book Group, 200 Madison Avenue, New York, N.Y. 10016. Published simultaneously in Canada
Printed in the United States of America
Designed by Christy Hale

Library of Congress Cataloging-in-Publication Data
Carter, Alden R.
Robodad / Alden R. Carter.
    p.   cm.
Summary: Fourteen-year-old Shar struggles to live a normal life as her father's mental instability, caused by an aneurysm of the brain, makes him more and more difficult as a family member.
[1. Mentally handicapped—Fiction.
2. Fathers and daughters—Fiction.
3. Family life—Fiction.]   I. Title.
PZ7.C2426Ro   1990   [Fic]—dc20   90-8179
CIP   AC
ISBN 0-399-22191-3
10 9 8 7 6 5 4 3 2 1
FIRST IMPRESSION

For the Roys:
Michel, Judy, Sylvie, Marc, and Alain

Chapter 1

I yelped and hopped across the family room on one foot. Sid and Alex looked up from their model starship. "She does that pretty good for a girl," Sid said. Alex grinned. I staggered to a chair and dug the plastic laser gun or rocket or whatever the heck it was from between my toes. I threw it at Sid as hard as I could, hoping for an eye or at least an ear. He caught it smoothly. "Thanks, Shar. We've been looking for that one." He handed it to Alex, who fitted it carefully onto a wing.

"Why don't you guys keep track of those darn things? God, a person can get maimed just walking around here."

"Why don't you wear shoes?" Sid said, not looking up from the plans.

I was about to let him really have it, but just then Dad came in from the kitchen with a can of pop and the big silver bowl he has for his snacks. He made for his chair in front of the TV, spilling Cheerios on the carpet and scattering a couple dozen model parts in his way. He didn't look back. Pepper padded after him, stopping long enough to eat the Cheerios and wag his tail at the boys.

Sid looked after Dad in disgust. "There goes RoboDad. Everybody out of the way, this guy don't give a shit." Alex laughed.

"Sid!" I snapped.

"Oops, and here's the caped avenger."

"Get in here!" I headed for the kitchen, so mad that I could hardly talk. After a few seconds, Alex got up and followed. Sid shrugged and climbed to his feet. I swung the door closed so that Dad wouldn't hear us—not that he'd pay any attention. "Look, you two. That guy in there is our Dad! Try to remember that, huh? Just because he's sick—"

Sid's face got red. "Hey, don't lay that crap on us, Shar. You're not the only one who remembers that he's our Dad!"

"Then why don't you treat him like it, huh?"

"Why should we? He doesn't care anymore. That guy don't give a shit and he ain't gonna start."

"I don't want to hear that, Sid! How do you know he's not—"

"Because that's what the doctors say. Or didn't you bother to listen? Now just get off our backs, Shar!" We stood glaring at each other. Alex started to say something, then decided against it and just stared at his feet. In the living room, Dad laughed at a cartoon on the TV, and suddenly there were big tears in my eyes. "Oh, crap," Sid said and turned away.

Alex handed me a napkin from the counter. "Come on, Shar. We still love Dad. It's just that—"

"It's just that he's not Dad anymore," Sid said. "He's just a big baby watching cartoons or baseball all day. He doesn't hear anything we say. Hell, he doesn't even notice us."

"Don't swear," I said.

Sid snorted. "You should talk."

Now I really wanted to cry. I'd been trying so hard to

keep everything running smoothly ever since Mom had put me in charge at home. But Alex and Sid wouldn't listen to me. Maybe fourteen didn't make me grown up or anything, but I sure as heck knew a lot more than a couple of twelve-year-olds. I wiped my nose and leveled my voice, trying to sound as much like Mom as I could. "Look, we've got to work together. If you guys could cooperate just a little—"

Sid groaned. Alex said, "Come on, Shar. Ease off a little, huh? It's not—"

Dad barged through the door. He brushed by us and started digging among the boxes of breakfast cereal. Sid and Alex looked at each other and made a quick exit. "What are you looking for, Dad?"

"Those little round ones with the holes."

"Cheerios?"

"Ya, Cheerios."

"I think you ate the last of them." He gave me an angry look. "But these are real good." I pulled out a box of Honey Bran Squares.

He stared at the box, then shoved in a big hand and pulled out one of the little squares. He eyed it suspiciously. "They're not round."

"I know, Dad, but they're real good."

He sniffed the square, then popped it in his mouth. He chewed, grunted, emptied the rest of the box into his big bowl, and left without another word. In the next room, Sid yelled, "Here he comes. Make way for Daddy."

I stared at the Cheerio dust and scattered bran squares on the counter, then got a rag and began cleaning up. Once upon a time, he'd been neat, always quick to help Mom in the kitchen and even quicker to raise an eyebrow at one of us kids if we slopped stuff around. But he didn't care anymore, just like he didn't care about most things. Including me.

Mom got home around eight, early for her. I was at the dining-room table, trying to mend a tear in my favorite jeans. "Hi, Mom. Sell a house?"

She glanced into the living room where Dad was lost in a Brewers game. "No, they wanted something less expensive. Tomorrow I'm going to show them that old brick one in the country." She hung up her light summer coat and sat down. She looked beat. "Did he eat anything for supper?"

"A hot dog and some beans. He's been on cereal since."

"Well, that can't hurt him. The boys behave themselves?"

I looked down and shrugged. "Ya, o.k. Sid got kinda lippy."

She watched my hands working on the rip. "You've got to make those stitches tighter. Here, let me show you."

She put on her glasses and started putting in those neat, tight stitches that I can never get quite right. "Mom, don't you think Dad's a little better this week? You know, like noticing more things?"

"Do you?"

"Well, maybe a little. At dinner, he talked some to the boys about the Cubs game. Somebody named Dawson hit three home runs." Mom bit off the end of the thread and picked up the spool. "Well, what do you think, Mom?"

She rethreaded the needle, taking a long minute before she answered. "I think he's a little better on some days than on others."

"But, Mom, if he starts having more good days, then maybe he'll begin to really get—"

Mom put the jeans in her lap and looked at me with her cool blue eyes. "Shar, you know what the doctors say. His physical condition is more or less stable, but there's no fixing the damage to his brain and no way for him to get better on his own. He's going to stay this way."

I was going to object that the doctors couldn't know everything, but then I looked into the next room and saw Pepper nudging Dad's limp arm with his nose. "Mom, it's happening again." Mom turned. Pepper sat back on his haunches, whined, and thumped his tail on the floor. Dad still didn't move. "I'll take Pepper out," I said.

"No, let Pepper wait. When he comes out of the black-out, we want everything to be the same."

Dad seemed to rouse himself. He looked at Pepper and then at the commercial on TV. "What happened? The Brewers had two on with nobody out." He turned to stare at us.

"Uh, I don't know, Dad. I wasn't watching."

"What do you mean you weren't watching? You're sitting right there, aren't you? I close my eyes for a second and nobody pays any attention to the game. Now how the hell am I supposed to know what happened? All I ask around here . . ."

His voice was rising fast and he started jumbling his words. Mom said quietly, "Shar, I think Pepper needs to go out."

I hopped up. "Let's go out, Pep."

11

We walked toward the nature preserve in the last of the light. The end of August and already the days were getting shorter and the nights cool. It made me a little sad to think of the leaves changing and fall coming. I'm a summer person, and summers hardly last anything in Wisconsin. A couple of years ago, we went to southern California at Christmastime. Palm trees, swimming, and Disneyland in December. Someday, I'm going to move out there just to get warm.

Ahead of me, Pepper snuffled in some grass and then started to roll in whatever smelled so good. "Give me a break, Pep. I just washed you last weekend." He paused long enough to grin at me, then started rolling again. "Come on, Pep. Let's run."

Pepper's nearly as old as the boys, and he doesn't romp or run much anymore. Sleeping is more his speed. But he had no trouble catching up to me. Sometimes I hate dogs; they make you look so darned foolish when you're running and they're just trotting along and grinning at you: "Hey, what's the matter, hippo butt. Got ya winded already?"

"Watch it," I said to him. "One more crack like that and no biscuits for breakfast." He grinned, then dropped back to smell around the foot of a mailbox. I slowed to a walk and tried to catch my breath. God, I was out of shape. Back in June I'd had big plans to lose ten pounds and get a decent tan. With a little help from Mother Nature, I might even get a boy to notice me this year. But here it was nearly time for school to start, and all I had to show for my summer plans were three or four more pounds on my butt, another inch of flab on my gut, and hardly anything added higher up, where so far Mother Nature had been pretty stingy. If Cindy came back from camp looking like a movie star, I'd kill myself.

We walked as far as the hill overlooking the lake, then turned back. Most of the lights were off when we got back to the house. I pushed open the door between the kitchen and the dining room to listen. I could hear the faint sounds of the baseball game playing on the small TV in Mom and Dad's bedroom. Mom said something and Dad grunted. Pepper pushed by me and went to lie on the rug outside their door.

I took a quick look in the fridge. I needed something low-cal. Like apple pie, maybe. Well, heck, I'd baked it, hadn't I? Besides the twins would probably eat the rest before I got another chance. I cut a wedge, poured a glass of milk, then made my way quietly to the stairs, praying that I wouldn't hear Dad start yelling: "Who's out there? Stop right where you are. Goddamn it, I've got a gun." I avoided the squeaky step halfway up, tip-toed past the twins' room, and slipped into my own room at the end of the hall. Safe.

I made space on my desk—God, I had to get this place cleaned up before school started on Tuesday—and sat down to eat my pie. On the lawn below my window, the square of light from Mom and Dad's bedroom winked out.

Until last spring, they'd slept upstairs in one of the real bedrooms, and the small room off the family room was Dad's den, where he kept his guns, fishing rods, bowling trophies, and stacks of *Field and Stream* and *Outdoor Life*. He didn't care so much for TV then, and you could find him in his den most evenings. When I was little, I used to spend a lot of time with him. You see, we were buddies. I love Mom and usually get along with her o.k., but until a few years ago the twins took up most of her time. Almost every night while she got them to bed, I'd spend an hour in the den with Dad. I'd color a picture or do a puzzle on his old desk while he worked on a gun or a rod. Or, I'd sit beside him, and he'd read me a book or tell me a story—he knew lots of funny stories then.

After I grew out of those things and the twins got older, Dad started doing more with them. But Dad and I were still buddies, and I didn't think anything could ever change that. Then one day, *wham*. A hemorrhage blew out part of his brain, and he stopped caring much about any of us. Now I think back to those hours we spent in his den, and I'd give anything in the world for just one more.

I try not to think too much about last spring and that little artery exploding in Dad's head and changing everything. But it's hard when I'm alone or with Dad or with people who don't seem to have any problems. In other words, just about all the time.

It happened on one of those wet, cold March days. Mom and I were getting supper on the table and wondering why Dad was late, when Phil Simonson called from the warehouse. Dad was shipping foreman then, and it was a darn good job. SuperComp makes just about the most advanced computers in the world, and you can't have some clumsy jerk boxing and shipping fifteen-million-dollar supercomputers. Dad used to brag that he could box a spider's web, ship it to Mongolia, and it would arrive without a thread broken. And I'll bet you he could have.

I hope Dad never finds out the details of that afternoon, but maybe it wouldn't make any difference to him now. Dad and three or four other guys were loading one of the new EN-2 models into a truck when Dad just keeled over and fell off the forklift. His foot came off the pedal and the forklift jerked forward, dumping the box off the loading dock. Even Dad hadn't packed it well enough for that. Cindy's dad works in repair, and he said that it took them three weeks and mucho bucks to fix the damage. Anyway, I guess there was quite a ruckus when the box hit, so it took a minute for anybody to notice that Dad was just lying on the concrete looking dead except for this faint trembling all over his body. They called an ambulance, and a while later somebody thought to call us.

When Mom put down the phone, she stood frozen for a moment. Then she was moving, all efficiency and self-control. "Kids, your dad got sick at the warehouse and he's in the hospital now. Alex, get my coat from the hall closet. Sid, my purse is on the dresser upstairs. Hop to it."

At the door, she said, "Now, Shar, you're in charge. I'll be back as soon as I can. Boys, you behave. And, Shar, call Bob Marston and tell him he's going to have to take that house-showing by himself." She hurried away through the cold drizzle that was turning to sleet in the March twilight. That was the first of a lot of nights I was in charge at home.

The doctors at the hospital didn't waste any time. Late that night, they sawed open Dad's skull to save his life. Alex, Sid, and I didn't get to see him until a couple of days later. He looked pretty much the same except for the bandages, but there was something missing from his eyes. He didn't say anything, just stared at us like he didn't recognize us and didn't much care either. We stood around the bed for a few minutes trying to act cheerful, then Mom told us to wait in the doctor's office down the hall.

I think that was about the only time I'd ever seen Sid cry. Even when he was little and fell off his bike, he'd get mad instead. Alex has always been the one to cry when his knees or elbows or feelings get scraped. But in the doctor's office, Sid sat in a chair by the window and cried. Alex and I tried to tell him that everything was going to be o.k., but he just waved us away. I think he'd guessed something about Dad that we'd missed.

Sid was all right by the time Mom and this big, balding doctor came in. Mom sat with her purse hugged to her stomach, looking scared and a whole lot older. The doctor cleared his throat and began giving us the facts.

He was a neurosurgeon, the kind of doctor who spends his life poking around people's brains and nervous systems. He started by showing us a chart of the brain with all these little arteries running through it, sort of like the branches of a tree. He pointed out the one that had swelled up and ruptured in Dad's head. "We clipped and sutured the artery and evacuated as much of the blood as possible. However, there was considerable asphyxiation of brain tissue in the vicinity." He looked at us uncertainly. "Uh, by that I mean that the blood drowned a large number of brain cells before we could do anything."

He cleared his throat again and flipped to a chart showing the brain in a patchwork of colored shapes. "Now there's a lot that we don't know about the human brain, but the mapping we've done indicates that most sections have quite distinct functions. For instance . . ." He started using a wooden pointer like he was giving a geography lesson. "Now the part of Mr. Zarada's brain that was affected by the hemorrhage is here. It controls a number of the higher emotions, for example an appreciation of music, art, or fine food." He hesitated. "We also think it's the part of the brain that controls much of our appreciation for special relationships—the bonds we make with friends and family."

He looked at Mom. "I'm sorry to tell you this, but you should expect some alteration in how Mr. Zarada views you and your children. He may no longer show much capacity for affection, parental concern, or . . . well, the word love would sum it up best, I guess."

Alex and I looked at Mom while Sid just glared at the chart. Mom let out a long slow breath. "Will he get better?" she asked.

The doctor put down the pointer slowly and sat on the edge of his desk. He studied his hands for a moment, and I tried not to think of how they'd spent hours inside my dad's skull. "I don't want to rule out the possibility. When there is damage to a part of the brain that controls an important function, we often see a healthy part of the brain gradually assume that function. However, I know of no case where another part of the brain has compensated for damage to this particular area. It doesn't appear that Mother Nature has assigned a very high priority to its functions." He sighed and straightened. "I'm sorry, Mrs. Zarada, but in all likelihood your husband will never regain those higher emotions."

He went on to give us a lot of details about the recovery time, therapy, and drugs Dad would need, but I didn't hear most of it. *Dad not loving us?* I didn't believe it. I wouldn't believe it. Dad would prove all the doctors wrong. And I was going to help him.

Five months later, I'm still looking for a way. I haven't given up like the twins have. Or the way I sometimes think Mom has. But so far I haven't been able to do a lot of good. Dad spends his days in front of the TV, and I can't get his attention a lot of the time. And when I do, it's usually because I've done something that makes him mad. He gets into these kind of childish tantrums real easy, and they frightened me a lot at first. The doctors warned us before we brought him home that he might even get violent—and that was scary because Dad is a real big guy—but the worst he's ever done is yell like . . . well, Sid said it, like a big baby.

The blackouts are scary though. Sometimes Dad will be saying something or walking across the room, and he'll just freeze. His eyes go glassy, and he'll be like that for a few seconds or even a minute or two. Then he'll go on like nothing happened. We've learned to behave as if the clock stopped for us too. Otherwise, he gets real confused and upset.

Because of the blackouts, Dad can't work or drive a car. Mom doesn't even want him climbing the stairs. That's why she decided to use his den as their bedroom. Alex, Sid, Cindy, and I did the moving after school on the Friday Mom was bringing him home from the hospital. We didn't have a lot of time and almost killed ourselves getting their mattress down the stairs, but we were waiting with streamers, horns, and party hats when they pulled into the driveway.

Dad came in leaning on Mom's arm. He didn't smile, just looked around like he was trying to remember the house and just who the heck these loud youngsters were. Mom got him in a chair, and Alex tried to perch a party hat on top of all the bandages wrapped around his head. "I'll get you some cake, Dad," I said.

I turned to get a piece of the cake that Cindy and I had baked the night before. Cindy was standing by the table, looking scared.

"Come on, Cindy," I whispered. "They're just bandages."

She tried to grin. "Ya, sure. It's just that I never thought he'd look like the invisible man on that miniseries. You know, where the guy unwrapped his head and there was nothing underneath the bandages."

Cindy's like that. About half the stuff in the world reminds her of some movie or miniseries she's seen. Last time we slept in a tent in the backyard, I practically had to gag her to keep from hearing about all the movies she'd seen where teenage girls got hacked to pieces in the middle of the night by maniacs with axes, chainsaws, and electric hedge trimmers. "Oh, shut up and cut the cake," I said. "You've got too much imagination."

"Ain't no such thing," she said.

Dad took a couple of bites of cake and then seemed to forget about it. I'd just given everybody else a second piece when I turned to find him staring at me. "Can I get you something, Dad?" He didn't reply, just kept staring at me with absolutely no expression on his face.

Mom put a hand on his arm. "Getting tired, dear? Maybe that's enough party until you've had a nap."

She gave his arm a little shake, and he finally came out of that trancelike stare. "Gotta pee first," he mumbled. Cindy started to giggle but caught herself.

"Come on, Alex," Sid said. "Let's go throw a ball around." They left.

Cindy and I started gathering up the plates, while Mom helped Dad to the bathroom. "Shar, I gotta get home," Cindy said. "I'll call you tomorrow morning."

"Why don't you just come over? We'll find something to do."

"Well, I don't know. Your dad might be sleeping late or something. Mom said I'm not supposed to go on acting like this is my home away from home. Not until he's better, you know."

I shrugged. "Not that much has changed. But o.k. Just don't forget to call, huh?"

Cindy left and I got some plastic wrap to put over the cake. Mom and Dad came out of the bathroom, and she led him toward the den. "Until you feel better, we'll sleep in the den. The kids got everything ready."

Dad came to a dead stop at the door. "Where's all my stuff?"

"Well, dear, there wasn't room for everything, so the kids put most of your sports things in the basement. They were careful; everything will be all right."

"I want my guns in here. And those . . . those tall gold things with little men on the top that I got for bowling."

"Trophies, dear."

"Ya, trophies. And my rods. I want my rods too."

"But, dear—"

He turned on her. "Here, not in somebody's basement! Here!"

"Dear, they're not in somebody's basement, they're in our own basement."

"Here, damn it. I want them right here!"

"All right, dear. All right. You lie down and take a nap on the couch, and the kids and I will get your things. Just come over here and lie down." She got him settled on the couch and sat on the floor by him, holding his hand. I got the rest of the party stuff to the kitchen.

Mom joined me a few minutes later. "I'm sorry, Shar. You kids did a great job, but I guess he needs familiar things around him right now. We'll move my dressing table and most of my clothes back upstairs and then get his things out of the basement."

"But, Mom, do you think he should have all those guns around? I mean he can't hurt himself with bowling trophies or fishing rods, but guns—"

"We'll lock all the shells away. Empty guns won't hurt him."

"But—"

"Shar, we're just going to have to make compromises until we know how he's going to react to things. If we can just get him sleeping in the den, then we won't have to worry about him falling on the stairs. Now go call the boys."

So we rearranged the den, and Dad never noticed that Mom had locked all the ammunition in a cupboard in the basement. As a matter of fact, he didn't pay any attention to his sports stuff for a long time after that.

We fell into a routine. Because Dad couldn't work and his disability checks weren't all that super, Mom started putting in all the hours she could. For years she's worked part-time for Bertleson Realty. She started as a secretary, but she got sick of doing paperwork for people not nearly as smart as she was. So she took a night-school course for her real-estate license, graduated at the top of her class, and became one of Bertleson's best agents. Being beautiful, charming, and wearing clothes like a model doesn't hurt either. (Got kind of a dumpy daughter, but you can't do everything right.) She likes her job, but it's frustrating when she works weeks and weeks for a sale only to lose it by a hair. That gets to her sometimes, especially now when she's got to get out there and be better than ever.

Because of Mom's work, I'm in charge at home most of the time. There's not anybody else available, since Mom's mother is the only one of my grandparents alive, and she lives in Florida with her new husband. Mom and Dad have friends, of course, but they're all busy people with families of their own. So, we have to make do pretty much on our own. I do the cooking and try to get the twins to do some of the cleaning. But Sid's impatient and Alex is so slow that he drives me nuts.

At first, they were pretty good at trying to interest Dad in things, especially the stuff he used to enjoy a lot, but it never worked out very well. Once they talked him into going fishing at the lake in the nature preserve. Sid was pretty put out when they got back. "I even had to bait his hook for him. Then he just sat there like he couldn't remember how to throw out a line. So, I did that for him. But the next time I turned around, he'd dropped the rod and wandered off to the end of the dock. He doesn't give a damn about fishing anymore. Hell, he doesn't give a damn about anything anymore."

"He seemed to like being in the sun though," Alex said. "He sat at the end of the dock with his feet in the water and this little smile on his face. I think he enjoyed it."

Sid grimaced. "Ya, kind of like a big potato plant just soaking up the rays."

"Sid," I said, "maybe it'll just take—"

But Sid didn't wait to hear me out. The door closed behind him, and I could see him walking back toward the lake with his head down and his hands deep in his pockets. Alex started digging in the refrigerator.

"Don't you think you'd better go after him?" I said.

"Na, he's o.k. Just disappointed. Don't worry about Sid, Shar. He was real patient with Dad. In a day or two, we'll take him fishing again."

They did try once or twice more, but it got harder and harder to talk Dad into anything. He was getting into his own routine of constant TV and endless snacks. After a while, Sid and Alex gave up.

They're really looking forward to school, and I guess

I am too. Mom plans to stay home most mornings, then get Dad all set for the afternoons when he usually sleeps some anyway. I'll get home as soon as I can after school to see if he's o.k. Mom says that I shouldn't worry so much and that I ought to give myself an hour with Cindy and my other friends first. But I think I'd be too nervous to have any fun until I'd at least looked in on Dad.

I scraped up the last of the pie crumbs with my fork. Maybe I should slip down to the kitchen for just a sliver more. Ya, and one of these days I'd have to start wearing a tent. Cool it, porkbelly. Time to wash up, read a little, and then get some beauty sleep—not that sleep's helped much in the past.

But instead of moving I sat for a while staring at the darkness beyond my window. I'd wanted a moon tonight—a big, orange, harvest moon—but there were too many clouds. And for some reason, that made me feel like crying. Come on, Shar, act your age. Better day tomorrow.

Chapter 2

"Hey, Sharzar!" Standing in the bright morning light, Cindy looked gorgeous. Oh, God.

I trotted down the steps. "Hey, Cindy. How's the happy camper?"

"Super. Ready to knock 'em dead."

"Uh, who?"

"The guys, dummy. You don't think I mean the teachers, do ya? Come on, or we'll be late."

We headed for school, dodging the grade-schoolers cluttering the sidewalks. I gave Cindy a closer look as she rattled on about her six weeks at camp. All my worst fears were confirmed. She was tan, fit, and *slender*. Her soft red-brown hair—hair that I'd kill to have instead of the curly black junk Mother Nature gave me as another one of her jokes—had bleached to a fiery blonde. God, the guys would be tripping over their tongues trying to get close to her.

"So how are things going in ol' New Bremen?" she asked.

"Huh? Oh, fine. Nothing much changed around here."

"Got any gossip?"

"Nothing I didn't write you about."

"Ya, in your whole three letters. Jeez, I thought you'd

died. Died or gotten a guy who didn't give you any time to write. Is there someone you ain't told me about, Sharzar?"

"Don't I wish. I just didn't have much to write about. I didn't get out much and things are about the same at home."

She hesitated. "Your dad's not any better, huh?"

"Well, sometimes I think he is." I started telling her some of the hopeful signs that I picked up now and then. But after a block, I noticed that she wasn't really listening. "So, anyway, it's slow, but I've still got a lot of hope."

"That's good. What classes do you—" A red Camaro whooshed by. Cindy craned her neck trying to get a better look through the back window. "Hey, was that Debbie Bauer?"

"Uh, it looked like some guy to me."

"Not driving, stupid. I mean *riding* with that guy."

"I didn't see."

"That's what I need—a guy with a red Camaro and money." She turned to look at me carefully. She frowned. "Is that the best outfit you could find for the first day at school?"

I glanced down at my blouse, jeans, and tennies. "I don't know. What difference does it make?"

Cindy groaned and flopped an arm across my shoulders. "Sharzar, listen to your big sister Cindy. First day is when all the guys are checking out the girls. You know, to see if last year's stick is now Ms. Volumptuous."

"Voluptuous. No m-sound," I said.

"Whatever. And so the girls—particularly the ones like us who ain't exactly ready for the pages of *Glamour*—have got to make the best use of what we've got. That or get ready for a long, cold, lonely winter."

"So I might as well start knitting mittens, huh?"

"Well, no. But you could've made a better start. Give me your brush, and I'll try to do something with your hair."

I didn't particularly want to stand on the sidewalk with half the world watching while Cindy tried to knock a little control into my hair. But there's not much point in arguing with her. I got the hairbrush from my purse, and she started dragging it through my curls. "God," she said. "Why didn't you spend a little time on this?"

"I did," I said sourly.

"It sure doesn't look like it. You've got a big rat's nest right here."

"Ouch! Hey, take it easy."

"Ya, ya. Well, that's better, I guess. Now tuck in your blouse tight. Gotta show off what you've got, girl."

"What there is of it."

"There's enough."

As ninth graders, we got to sit at the back of the auditorium during assembly, staring down toward the stage over all the rows of eighth and seventh graders. We got a little rowdy and got yelled at. But, hey, a little bit of rowdy came with the territory.

The rest of the day we had shortened classes for getting books, course outlines, and stuff. Nearly every teacher said something about how we should set a good example for the younger kids and work hard to get ready for high school next year. That got to be a bit of a yawner. First day of school was for seeing other kids, not for worrying about studying or the distant future. I ran into Sid and Alex between first and second periods.

They looked very pleased to be in junior high at last. Whoa, big thrill, guys. Just don't let on you're related to me, huh? I ducked into my algebra class.

I had pretty good friends in most of my classes, but I was disappointed that the computer had put Cindy in all different sections. I looked for her at lunch, but for the first time in years, we didn't even have that together. Crap. Well, maybe I could take Mom's suggestion and spend some time with her after school. I sat down to eat with some other girls, and suddenly a weird thought crossed my mind: maybe Cindy would be glad that we didn't have lunch or any classes together. For a moment the thought made me almost ill. Oh, come on, Shar, I told myself. You've been best friends since first grade; nothing's changed just because she looks great and you look awful. I stared at my half-eaten sandwich. Maybe I ought to start skipping lunch.

"Earth calling Shar. Earth calling Shar."

"Huh?" I looked up to see Pam Corvitz grinning at me. A couple of other girls giggled.

"Jeez, you're really out of it, Sharzar. Who you thinking about?"

"Nobody."

"Come on, you can tell us."

"No one. Really."

"Likely story. So, what's your next class?"

I made a face. "Biology."

"Ya, me too. Ugh, right after lunch."

"Better than right before," Meg Heywood said. "Come in with your hands smelling of that formaldehyde junk and then try to eat a sandwich. My brother says that he almost blew his tubes when he tried to eat a tuna-fish sandwich after dissecting a crab. He said that the insides looked just the same. He hasn't eaten tuna fish since."

I didn't really want to hear any more about puking or biology, but I sat listening to horror stories until the bell rang for the next period. Pam and I walked to the biology room together, making sick jokes about dissecting and tuna-fish sandwiches.

I like school most of the time and was looking forward to all my classes except biology. But something else was worrying me a lot more than biology or the crazy thoughts I'd had about Cindy. This would be Dad's first afternoon alone. Suppose he tried to cook something and got burned. Or suppose the house caught on fire. Or suppose . . .

And I complain about Cindy having too much imagination. By the time I got through biology and made it to my last class, all I could do was stare at the clock and try not to invent too many more supposes.

"Ms. Zarada . . ."

"Huh? Oh, yes, Mr. Lauerman."

"Glad to see you're with us. Your book number, please."

Blushing, I flipped open the cover. "Seventy-eight."

"Not the history text, Ms. Zarada. This is English." The class laughed.

"Uh, right. Yes, sir. Uh, one hundred and four."

"Thank you. All right, class. For next time, I want you to read . . ."

I copied down the assignment, wishing that my face would cool down. Heck of a start, Shar.

After the last bell, I waited on the front steps for Cindy. She didn't come right away, and I had that sick feeling again. We'd walked home together every day since first grade, but maybe that was all over. God, she couldn't have found a guy already. Oh, yes she could. I stared at my tennis shoes, where the big toe of my right foot had found a hole and was trying to wiggle out. If Cindy didn't show in five minutes, I'd—

"Hey, Sharzar! Over here." Cindy was waving from a knot of kids by the far door.

I felt a wave of relief and trotted over to join them. Cindy was in her element, making everybody laugh and looking just fantastic. They were mostly girls, but there were a couple of guys too and I could see how they were watching her. Mark Olson glanced my way. "Hi, Shar. How's it going?"

"Fine," I said. "How are—" But he'd turned away and was laughing at Cindy's story. And a second after I'd felt great, I knew that I really was going to lose her. She'd get a guy and I'd never, ever . . .

I felt tears start to blur my eyes and took a step back. Will you shut up, Shar? You are behaving like a jerk. Now snap out of it. Just pay a little attention to your hair tonight and wear something better tomorrow. I bit my lip and stepped back into the circle. I smiled at Mark—who didn't notice—and made like I was enjoying Cindy's camp stories as much as everyone else. But I had to watch the others to know when to laugh. Suppose Dad had . . .

I glanced at my watch. "Cindy, I gotta go."

"Oh, o.k."

I was half a block away when she caught up. "Jeez, did you have to take off right that second? I had to give them the punch line. Couldn't just leave my audience standing there."

"I'm sorry. I wasn't sure you were coming."

"Well of course I am. We've always walked home together. What's with you today?"

I shrugged. "I don't know. I'm just on edge. Maybe I'm getting my period early. You know, that PMS stuff."

"Ya, hormones going crazy. Hormones are history. Or is it future? What is that saying?"

"Hormones are important."

Cindy frowned. "No, that doesn't sound like it at all. Hey, do boys have hormones?"

"Of course they do. What do you think testosterone is?"

"Teswhatzit? What the heck is that?"

It was my turn to groan and flop a sisterly arm across her shoulders. "Look, Ms. Fashion Plate, I think you'd better know what you're getting into." I gave her some scientific details.

Her eyes got a little wider and she giggled. "How do you know all that stuff?"

"I read books. You might try it sometime."

"And miss all the surprises? I'll wait until it's a miniseries. I can see it now: *Testosterone meets Godzilla*. Who is mightier? The crazed male hormone or the monster that ate Tokyo?"

Another day I might have given her the girl-you-are-very-weird look, but suddenly it felt just like old times and we started laughing so hard that we had to hold onto each other to keep from falling down. Some gradeschoolers edged carefully to one side to let the crazy people pass.

Cindy caught her breath. "God, that felt good. I missed you, Shar. Most of those girls at camp didn't have any sense of humor. Real preppie types, you know: 'Oooo, what color polish should I put on my toenails to match Daddy's BMW?' I had to wait to get back here to be a little strange."

I grinned. "I missed you too. There haven't been a whole lot of laughs around . . ." I let that trail off. Shut up, Shar. Don't spoil things by getting serious now.

We walked for a minute or two in silence. "So how'd school go?" Cindy asked.

"O.k. How about you?"

"Great. Classes look easy and the place is crawling with real honest-to-God boys. What more could you ask? Hey, let's drop off our books at my house and go downtown."

"I don't know if I should."

"Oh, come on. Everybody'll be down there."

"I gotta see how Dad is."

She hesitated. "Ya, of course. Well, we can leave our books at your house instead. . . . So, did you meet any new guys or any old guys with new ideas?"

"Not very many. How about you?"

"Oh, a possibility or three. I'm still looking for the guy with the red Camaro, though. A guy with wheels and money, that's what I want."

"Suppose he's a pervert."

"Depends how perverted. Hey, do you remember that movie where the guy's car takes possession of his brain and is making him do all sorts of weird things? So his girl . . ." Cindy was off and I let her rattle on, while I kept my eyes on the sky above our neighborhood for signs of smoke and flame.

The house was still standing. "Come on in," I said. "We'll grab a pop while I change this blouse."

"Uh, I'm not thirsty. I'll just stay out here on the porch and work on my tan." I glanced at her sharply.

She gave me a sheepish grin. "Well, he might be sleeping or something."

"Right," I said.

Dad was watching cartoons, Pepper stretched out at his feet. "How you doing, Dad?"

He turned to look at me. "Where is everybody?"

"Mom's at work. The twins should be home from school soon. Do you need anything?"

"Ya, some of that fruit stuff." He held out his plastic cup, his stare back on the television screen.

"Kool-Aid?"

"Ya. Kool-Aid."

I got him some, then called Mom at work. "Hi, Mom. Dad seems o.k., and the boys are going to be home soon. Is it all right if I go downtown with Cindy?"

"That's fine, dear. I told you not to worry so much."

"I just wanted to check."

"Go ahead and have fun. How's Cindy?"

"Fine. She looks real good." Of course, I may have to kill her for that, but . . . "Uh, Mom, could you give me a few bucks? I want to buy a new pair of jeans."

"About time, I'd say. Come by the office. But you'll have to hurry; I've got a showing at four-thirty."

I ran upstairs, slipped into a better blouse, tucked it in tight, then stood sideways for a quick look in the mirror. Well almost enough, anyway. Downstairs again, I looked in on Dad—no change—then beat it out the back door. "Let's get going before the twins get home or they'll tag along," I said.

"Right," Cindy said. "Death to all twelve-year-olds."

Mom was over by the coffee machine on the far side of the office talking to a tall guy in a snappy blue blazer.

She saw us and waved. Cindy whistled through her teeth. "Who's the hunk?"

"Bob Marston. He works with Mom. He's too old for you."

"I know that, but does he have any kids? Like sons, you know."

"Two in college. They're too old for you too."

"Darn. I'll bet they're gorgeous."

"Ya, they are."

Bob must have told Mom a pretty good joke, because she was giggling hard and had to wipe her eyes. Bob grinned, gave her arm a pat, and headed for the door. "See you at seven," he called to her. He gave us a toothy smile as he passed. "Hi, girls."

Mom came over, still smiling at whatever Bob had said. She handed me two twenties. "I want to see change *and* receipts." I was offended and it showed. "Just kidding, dear. Buy what you need. Hi, Cindy. Camp agreed with you; you look great."

"Thanks, Mrs. Z. You look good too. But you always do."

"Well, *thank you,* Cindy." She glanced at her watch. "I've got to run. You girls have a good time."

Outside, Cindy said, "Well, she's certainly chippy."

"*Chippy?* Where do you get that stuff, Cindy?"

"It was big with the yuppie girls at camp. Hey, what's wrong now, Shar?"

"Nothing!" I snapped.

"Well, o.k. Then sound like it, huh?"

I grumped an apology.

At Penney's I found some good-looking jeans, while Cindy salivated over some sweaters that were way out of our range. But in the changing room, I had to take a deep breath to get the jeans buttoned. Crap, had I gained that much weight? Maybe they were just cutting them different.

When I tossed the jeans back on the pile, Cindy said, "Hey, I thought those looked pretty good. On sale too."

"I want to look a couple of other places. There are a lot of sales now. Let's get a Coke first."

We bought our Cokes at the taco stand down the mall a ways. A male voice yelled, "Hey, Cindy!"

We turned to see Mark Olson and three other guys. "Well, how-do," Cindy said. She brushed back a strand of her red-gold hair and laid on a big smile.

"How-do to you too," Mark said, demonstrating his usual wit. I grimaced. Still, he was pretty hunky, even if he was too young to own a Camaro. Mark and two of the other guys crowded in around Cindy, a bunch of junior Bob Marstons, all acting too cool by about half. I'd never liked Bob, not even when he used to bring his family over for cookouts in our backyard. That was before his wife, Janet, died real young of cancer. I'd liked her and felt bad, but it hadn't changed my feelings about Bob.

"Uh, nice weather, huh?"

I turned to see Paul O'Neil. I'd hardly noticed him among the others, but Paul has always been pretty easy to miss, even though he's not a bad-looking guy or anything. "Oh, hi, Paul. Sorry, I didn't catch that."

"I said the weather's nice."

"Ya, I guess."

"If it stays this way through February, we'll have it licked."

"What licked?"

"The winter."

"Oh." I looked back at Cindy and her little crowd of admirers. Ya, little Bob Marstons. He looked at Mom the same way, and I didn't like that one damn bit.

"So, uh, do your classes look o.k.?" Paul asked.

"Ya, everything but biology."

"Why biology? I heard Munrow's a pretty good teacher."

"I don't like doing cruel things to worms and frogs and getting my hands icky."

"Oh. Well, maybe we could be lab partners. I could do most of the work."

I glanced at him. "Are you in that class?"

"Ya, a couple of rows over from you."

"Sorry, I didn't notice."

"Oh." He shuffled. "Well, I think you're allowed to choose lab partners. What do you say?"

"I'll think about it. Hey, Cindy. I'm going down to Prange's to look at jeans. Meet me there, huh? See you, Paul."

"Ya, sure," he said.

I'd just rejected another tight pair of jeans when Cindy waltzed into the clothing department. "Well, how do you like them apples? Got a date first day."

"Terrific," I said, holding up another pair and wincing at the size of the waist. "Which one?"

"Mark. He needs some work, but I think I can train him."

"I didn't know you did brain surgery. Darn, I can't find anything cut right. Let's try somewhere else."

Outside, Cindy asked, "Why'd you walk off on Paul? Don't you like him?"

"I don't know. I never thought about it."

"Looks like he grew three inches and put on ten pounds of muscle over the summer. He's a pretty good-looking guy these days."

"I didn't really notice."

She reached out and spun me to face her. "What is with you today?"

I stared at her. God, she was really angry! "Uh, what do you mean?"

"You know what I mean. You come to school looking like a wreck. After school you walk off like you hardly know me. Down here you nearly bite my head off when I say your mother looks chippy. And when *I* get a date, you say: 'Oooo, terrific. But he needs brain surgery.'"

"I'm sorry, Cindy. I—"

"I'm not finished. And when Paul—who I've always thought was a pretty nice guy—shows a little interest in Shar Zarada, you treat him like he's got leprosy or something."

I looked at her in astonishment. "Come on. Paul's not interested in me. What gave you that idea?"

"I've got eyes, dummy. He ignores me and starts hanging around you, trying to make conversation. If he wasn't interested, he would have gone across to Musicland or something."

"I guess I didn't notice."

"Well, wake up and start noticing things, huh? And you might start by noticing that I've got some feelings too, and your *terrific* sarcasm doesn't make 'em feel real good!" She turned on her heel and headed for the exit.

I hesitated a moment, then hurried after her. I trailed a step behind as she strode across the parking lot in the warm sunshine. Finally, I said, "I'm sorry, Cindy. I'm really happy you got a date. I've just been feeling bitchy recently. Ignore me. I'll get over it."

After a few more steps, she sighed and slowed down so I could catch up. She patted my shoulder a couple of times. "Ya, I get that way too sometimes. You need friends to give crap to now and then. That and for borrowing money from. By the way, could you lend me fifty bucks?"

I laughed. "Sure. But I get Mark."

"Even if he needs a brain overhaul?"

"Oh, he's not so bad. I guess I'm just jealous."

"You can have him when the guy with the red Camaro shows up."

"It's a deal. Do you want the fifty now?"

"No. Hold onto it. I won't forget."

After a block, I said, "Do you really think Paul was interested in me?"

"Ya, I kind of thought so. I mean, neither of us have a whole lot of experience, but it kind of looked that way to me."

"I guess I really blew it."

"Oh, just smile at him in class tomorrow. If he's really interested, he'll try again."

"Maybe," I said, not feeling very hopeful.

I heard the baseball smacking into gloves outback and knew that the twins had talked Dad into a game of catch. That's about the only activity that doesn't take a lot of convincing these days. I got some water on the stove for spaghetti, then looked out the family-room window. They were in a triangle, the ball a white blur between them. Alex dropped the ball and Dad frowned, but Alex scooped it smoothly off the grass and fired an off-balance hummer to Sid. Dad grinned. I went back to making supper.

I was about to call them when Mom pulled into the driveway. She came in hurriedly, glancing at her watch. "I've got to rush. Bob and I have a showing at seven, and I've got to get over there to talk to the sellers for a few minutes first. Supper almost ready?"

"Soon as I get the spaghetti sauce hot and call the guys."

"Spaghetti?" She looked down at her beige suit. "Oh, rats. I'm not going to risk having to change. Bob and I'll grab a sandwich after the showing." She headed for the stairs. "I've got to check my face."

"You look fine, Mom." I peeked at the garlic bread under the broiler, then went to call Dad and the twins.

Not bad, even if the sauce did come out of a jar and the spaghetti was a little underdone. I reached for a second helping. "Why don't you settle for one," Sid said. "You're getting fat."

I stared at him, so surprised that I couldn't think of anything to say. Then I exploded. "I'll eat what I want to! I do everything around here and all you do is criticize. If you don't like how I do things, then do them yourself!" I jumped up and ran for the stairs. Dad watched me go with vague curiosity.

Sid said, "I didn't say anything about how she does things. I just said she was getting fat."

Alex said, "Well, you might have—"

I slammed the door of my room on all three of them.

Mom didn't get home until nearly ten. I was propped up on my bed reading the English assignment when she looked in. "Everything o.k.?" she asked.

"I haven't noticed. I've been up here since supper."

"Another spat with Sid?"

"Ya, you could call it that. Or you could just say that Sid's a jerk. An ungrateful, lippy, sarcastic little jerk. That's the way I'd put it."

"That bad, huh?"

"I'm being kind," I said. "He's worse than that."

Mom sat down on the end of my bed and sighed. "I really wish you kids would try—"

"Hey, don't blame me, Mom. I try. I put together a pretty good supper, and everybody seemed to enjoy it, even Dad. Then what does Sid say? 'Hey, porker, lay off the spaghetti. You're getting fat.'"

"He didn't really call you a 'porker,' did he?"

"Well, not exactly, but he said I was getting fat." Mom watched me, not saying anything. I shifted uncomfortably and looked down at the book on my lap. "I mean, I know I've put on a couple of pounds, but I don't need some twelve-year-old telling me."

She nodded. "I'll talk to him. Sid's got to work on his manners."

"And tell Alex that he could back me up once in a while, instead of always sticking up for Sid."

"Well, I guess he's just used to that. I'll talk to him too." She stood and leaned over to kiss me on top of the head. "Don't stay up too late."

She was at the door when I remembered. "Mom, could you make sure I'm up by six-thirty? I want to do something with my hair."

"Sure. I'll help if you want me to."

Chapter 3

I'd intended to give Paul a big smile when I took my seat in biology, but my courage evaporated. All I could manage was a faint "Hi, Paul," then looked away quickly, unsure if he'd even heard me.

I spent an hour on my hair again the next morning, then stood in front of the mirror for five minutes telling myself: Be confident, darn it. You're gorgeous—or at least not the absolute pits. Now give him a big smile and a big "Hiya, Paul." It didn't work. I took one look at him and my mouth froze. I think my hair fuzzed into a big ball too. He smiled and said, "Hi," but I was so tongue-tied that I only gave him a sickly grimace that probably looked like I had a stomachache.

Thursday, I rolled over and slept through my date with my curls. I packed a five-pound lunch while I waited for Cindy. To heck with it. Paul had just wanted to talk about the weather—a budding meteorologist or something equally boring. That afternoon Mark walked home with Cindy. I trailed behind, feeling like a walking dumpster in three or four different ways.

An overturned pitcher lay on the counter, Kool-Aid dripping over the side to a sticky orange puddle on the floor. A blackout had probably conked Dad in the middle of pouring. I got out the mop, feeling a little like

Cinderella cleaning up after sloppy stepsisters. Here, handsome prince. Here, boy. Come get me out of here.

I came down for breakfast Saturday morning, wondering when Cindy would call with news about her big date. I half hoped that Mark had acted like a jerk. Mom was at the waffle iron. "Beautiful day," she said. "It looks like we're going to have a little more summer."

I grunted—I'm not a morning person even under the best circumstances—and glanced through the window at the thermometer beside the bird feeder. Nearly seventy degrees. "Dad up yet?" I asked.

"He's out in back looking at the boat."

"Oh? Why?"

"I don't know. You remember how he used to love that boat. I guess he just thought of it again. Watch this waffle; I'm going to call the boys."

I drank orange juice and watched the waffle, wondering why Dad had the sudden interest in the boat. He'd taken it out of storage to get it ready for the summer only a week before he'd fallen off the forklift, but I didn't think he'd glanced at it since. The back door opened, and he came through the kitchen, walking very deliberately, and disappeared into the basement. What the hey?

We were nearly done with breakfast when he came back up the stairs. He looked at Sid and Alex. "Let's go waterskiing."

Their mouths dropped about a foot, and they both looked quickly at Mom, who held a bite of waffle suspended halfway between plate and mouth. "Uh, gee, Dad," Sid said. "Isn't it kinda late in the year for waterskiing?"

"Why? It's warm enough!" His voice was sharp.

Mom glanced at me, then said to him, "Well, maybe tomorrow, dear. I've got to work until late afternoon and—"

"I want to go waterskiing today. I haven't had the boat out all summer!" His lower lip twitched into an angry pout.

"But, dear," Mom said. "It's twenty miles to Tall Pine, and we'd have to launch the boat and unhitch the trailer before I could start back for town. I just don't have the time."

"Aren't you working with that Marston guy again?"

"Well, yes—"

"O.k., then you go with him, and we'll drive to the lake."

I'd been dreading this. In the months since he'd come home from the hospital, Dad had never questioned why Mom did all the driving. But he'd never acknowledged his blackouts either, and no one had guts enough to tell him that he *couldn't* drive.

Mom hesitated a long moment. "Well, I would like a drive in the country before work. Just to see the leaves starting to change. Bob could pick me up at the lake and drop me off in the afternoon."

"Just don't take too long; I'm just about ready." He turned abruptly and disappeared into the basement.

Mom looked at the twins. "Go help your dad get the waterskiing things out of the basement."

They went, looking worried. The second they were out of earshot, I said, "Mom! You can't let us go alone. Suppose something happens?"

"Nothing is going to happen. You're all excellent swimmers." She went to the phone.

"Maybe Dad's forgotten."

"He hasn't forgotten. You never forget how to swim. You know that."

"But, Mom, I can't be—"

She stopped halfway through punching out Bob's number and gave an exasperated sigh. "Shar, aren't you the one who's always saying that we have to get him interested in things?"

"Yes, but—"

"So now he's interested in doing something. Why don't you accept that, be happy, and stop complaining? O.k.?" She fixed me with her laser-beam stare.

I nodded glumly, and she went back to calling Bob.

Bob showed up a half hour later, all full of smiles and fakey good cheer. Dad didn't object when Mom got behind the wheel of our car.

"Want to ride with me, Shar?" Bob asked. "Make sure I don't get lost?"

I wish you would, I thought. Permanently. "O.k.," I said.

We followed Mom, Dad, and the twins into the country. "How's your mother doing these days?" Bob asked.

"Fine," I said. Heck, you see a lot more of her than we do.

"She always seems great at the office, but I worry about her. It must be quite a strain at home."

Stay out of our business, you jerk. "We do o.k."

"Good. Your mom's one heck of a saleswoman. You should be proud of her."

I glared at him. "I *am* proud of her. We all are."

"That's good." He smiled, completely missing the sharpness in my voice. "So how's your dad doing?"

"About the same."

"Well, he looks good. Put on a few extra pounds." He

laughed. "But that's a problem a lot of us have. Middle-aged spread."

I grunted. Try teenage spread if you want problems. He started whistling softly, his eyes on the blacktop road winding through the trees just beginning to change from green to yellow, red, and orange.

Dad used to whistle a lot. He could whistle so loud that Pepper would hear him a quarter mile away. Or he could whistle low and sweet, never missing a note of any song you wanted to name. But he hadn't whistled a bar since the day he fell off the forklift. Instead, he hummed. You didn't pick it up unless you were real close to him, but you could feel it even when you didn't hear it—a soft, tuneless hum way out on the edge where only dogs and small soft-footed animals hear clearly.

"Mr. Marston, would you mind not whistling? It kind of hurts my ears."

"Huh? Oh, sure. No problem." He glanced at me. "Why'd you call me Mr. Marston? Heck, you've known me all your life, and I've always been just Bob to you kids."

I shrugged. "Just felt like it, I guess." I pointed down the road. "You've got to take the next left."

Mom backed the trailer down the ramp, and we got the boat off and floating free. She parked the car, then handed me the keys. "Keep these out of sight. Now, you're in charge, Shar. If he insists on driving the boat, you or one of the twins stay close to the controls. You can always reach over and throw it out of gear if he has trouble."

"Mom, I'm scared."

She glanced at the twins and Dad rigging the ski line.

"Everything will be all right. I think he could drive that boat in his sleep. Besides, there won't be many other boats on the lake today."

Bob called, "Leslie, we'd better get going."

Mom waved to him, then gave me a smile and a pat on the shoulder. "We'll be back between four and four-thirty. Try to have a good time. Everything will be fine." She hurried off, leaving me feeling abandoned. I looked quickly to see if Dad was watching, then put the car keys out of sight on top of the right front tire.

All morning, everything did go fine. I hadn't seen Dad so happy or so much his old self since the aneurysm. He wanted to drive right from the start, so I sat near him, ready to grab for the shift. But he handled the boat like a pro, and I started to relax. Sid and Alex took turns on the skis. They're both real good, and Dad grinned whenever he turned to watch one of them whizzing over the water.

But when I finally took a turn, I made my usual hash of things. I came to the surface after flopping for the third time to find Dad glaring at me. "I'll get it this time," I yelled. "Just give me one more try." Alex grinned and waved, but Sid looked only a little less disgusted than Dad. I got back onto the skis, angled them carefully, and braced my legs. Come on, girl. You can't let a couple of twelve-year-olds show you up every time. I took a deep breath, waved, then clamped both hands on the bar. Dad hit the gas, and the surge pulled me out of the water. For a terrible second I thought I was going to dump again, but then I was all the way up and skimming along.

I didn't try anything fancy, but just followed the wake until, after a couple of wide, easy circles, Dad throttled back and I settled slowly into the water. I was a little disappointed that he hadn't let me keep going a little longer, but at least I'd gotten up. Next time, I'd wow 'em.

We ate sandwiches in the shelter of an island in the middle of the lake, then lazed in the sun for an hour. The boys tried for pan fish but didn't have any luck, which made me just as glad since I didn't want any wet fish flopping around in the boat while I was taking a snooze. Through nearly closed eyes, I could see a few puffy clouds sliding across the bright blue sky as the boat bobbed in a fresh breeze. I felt good. To heck with Cindy, Mark, and Paul. I'd be o.k. Dad would be o.k. Everything would work out.

Something brushed my thigh. I moved my leg and settled myself more comfortably. But that something brushed my thigh again. A hand. I opened my eyes to see Dad staring intently at my skin. "What is it, Dad?"

"Like sandpaper," he said.

I tried to laugh. "I guess I need to shave." I sat up, pulling my legs under me. He looked into my eyes with that strange stare I'd first caught him giving me at the party the day he'd come home from the hospital.

Behind me, Sid cleared his throat. "Hey, the wind's starting to come up. Let's get in some skiing while we can."

Alex said, "Ya, I want to drive."

Dad turned around in his seat and took the wheel. "I'm driving; it's my boat." The twins looked at each other and shrugged.

Sid tossed the skis overboard. "I guess it's your turn, Shar. Then me, then Alex. But do something this time, huh? I get bored just watching you."

That hurt, but I didn't let it show. "I don't feel like getting wet just yet. You go ahead."

Alex is a good skier, but Sid is better, probably because he tries harder and takes more risks. Dad opened it up, and Sid rocketed along, swinging out to jump the waves thrown up by the big ninety-horse Johnson. Dad grinned and pushed the throttle open another notch. In the stern Alex cheered and pumped his fist in the air. Sid balanced far out on the end of the towline, his face fierce with concentration. Dad swung the boat, and Sid leaned hard against the turn to cross the boat's wake. Dad looked back, then cranked the wheel even tighter. I felt trouble coming, but my hand grabbed for the wheel a second too late. Sid tumbled, his skis flying high in the air as he smashed headlong into the wake.

Dad throttled back and swung in toward the spot where Sid lay limp, his head and shoulders held up by the life vest. Dad cut the engine to an idle thirty or forty feet from him. Alex yelled, "Hey, Sid. Are you o.k.?" Sid didn't respond, just rolled slowly over on his face.

"Dad, he's hurt," I screamed. "Get over there!" But Dad just sat watching Sid bobbing face down in the water.

I lunged for the controls, but he blocked me with a big arm. "I'm driving."

"Dad, you've got to get over there! Sid—your son— he's drowning." Dad stared at me without expression. "Dad, please—" I begged, but there was no response in his eyes and no time to argue. I jumped up. Alex was trying to throw the life ring to Sid, even though Sid was much too far away and unconscious anyway. "Stay with Dad," I yelled, threw off my bulky life jacket, and dove overboard.

I'm not the world's greatest swimmer, but the dive carried me half the way to Sid. I came to the surface, and for a terrible moment, I couldn't find him amid the choppy waves. Then I spotted the orange of his vest. I stroked for all I was worth. Ahead I could see his slender legs. I dove just beneath the surface, kicked hard, and had him by the ankles. I rolled him over and got an arm across his chest. Blood ran from a big bruise above his ear. I tried to shake him. "Sid, can you hear me?"

He choked, vomited water, and groaned. "My head," he said. His hand went to the bruise then fell back in the water.

"It's o.k. Just a bruise. I think one of the skis hit you." I choked on a mouthful of water and treaded water harder. "Sid, you've got to kick." I shook him again. "Please, Sid, I can't do it all by myself." He groaned but started kicking weakly. I stroked with one hand, my other gripping the loop at the back of his life vest. Far away, Alex stood waiting with the life ring. "Just keep kicking," I gasped. Alex threw the ring and it plopped ten feet from my nose. Just a few more strokes, just a couple more, just one . . .

The engine roared to life. I screamed "Dad," my mouth filling with water as I lunged for the life ring. Dad threw the boat into forward and hit the gas. In the stern, Alex staggered and fell as the bow lifted and my clawing fingers just managed to grab the ring. The shock of the line tightening nearly tore my arm from my shoulder and the dead weight of Sid pulled me under. For a moment, we fishtailed crazily, the swing rolling Sid over so that the loop on the back of his vest wound around my fingers. The pain was awful. I tried to scream, but a gallon of water choked me. I let go of the life ring and fought to free my other hand. Sid was coughing and thrashing, every movement mangling my fingers. I grabbed him by the hair, and he yelped as I pulled him toward me. "Stop," I yelled. "Just lie still." He did, and I managed to wrench my fingers free.

I hugged Sid against me and started treading water again. I was gasping with pain and exertion and my eyes were blurry with lake water and tears. I tried to spot our boat but couldn't find it on the vacant sheet of sunlit water beyond the settling wake. "Where'd they go?" Sid sobbed. "Why'd they leave us?"

"It's o.k., Sid. They're coming right back." I was praying: Please, Alex. Make him stop. Make him turn around. I twisted, searching desperately for other boats. Nothing. Just empty blue water all the way to the pines on the shore far away. I couldn't make it that far, not towing Sid through the choppy waves. God, was I really going to die a virgin? Heck, I'd never even been kissed decently—or indecently, for that matter. Oh, God.

In the distance, the roar of the big Johnson died. I craned my neck and spotted our boat against the glare of sun on water. Dad had stopped maybe two hundred feet away, and Alex was leaning over the side, trying to reach something in the water. The motor started up again, and Dad swung the boat into a long turn and began weaving slowly back and forth.

"The skis!" Sid groaned. "The jerk went looking for the skis."

"Hush," I said. "Save your strength." Should I wave? I wasn't sure. My legs were tiring and I felt a cramp start to creep up a thigh. I lay back and kicked to the side, trying to work it out. The boat stopped again, and Alex leaned over to pick up the other ski.

"Shar, he's crazy," Sid gasped, his eyes squeezed tight

against the sun and the pain of his bruise. "He was going too fast. Way too fast. And I knew it. But I wanted to show him that I could make that jump. God, what a stupid—"

"Just don't think about it now. We've got to hold on." Again the engine started, and finally, Dad steered toward us.

Alex was trying hard not to cry as he helped us in. "Dad wouldn't listen," he whispered. "Just saw that first ski drifting away and took off. I tried, guys. I really did."

"Who's next?" Dad said.

We stared at him. "Alex, stay with Sid," I whispered. I went to Dad. "Uh, Dad, I think we're kind of tired. And Sid's got a bump on his head. Maybe we ought to go back to the landing now."

He glared at me, then turned to Alex. "Come on, Alex. You need the practice. You're not half as good as Sid."

Alex looked down. "I'm, uh, real tired, Dad. I'm sorry."

"Well, how about you, Sid? You ready to try again?" Sid didn't even look at him. Dad's face went red. "You wimps," he snarled. He jammed the shift into forward so hard that the boat shuddered. I barely had time to grab hold of the back of the seat next to him. We pounded over the water at top speed. Ahead a floating log barely broke the surface. I started to scream, but Dad flicked his wrist and we missed it by inches.

Once upon a time, he would have stopped to tie a rope around that log so we could tow it ashore. He'd cared about other people then, even strangers who would never know the favor he'd done them as they

50

roared over the lake. But he didn't even slow now. He sat high on the back of his seat, eyes slitted against the wind blowing his thinning hair. And suddenly he grinned. But it wasn't like any grin that I remembered. Not sunny and gentle, but wolfish and hard. And I didn't know him anymore.

My fingers ached but I could still use them. I started helping Alex get the gear out of the boat, while Sid wobbled over to a tree and sat down with his head in his hands. Dad walked up the beach a dozen feet, unzipped his fly, and took a long leak on the sand. "God, did you see that, Shar?" Alex whispered. "He didn't even check to see if there were any people around."

"I saw," I said.

Alex choked back tears. "Shar, I'm really scared. When's Mom going to get here?"

"Soon. Don't cry. Don't do anything that'll get him upset." I glanced again at Dad. He'd walked up to the car and was leaning over to reach into the wheel well. My heart stopped. "Oh, my God. He saw where I put the keys."

We stood frozen while Dad walked around the car and got in. "What do we do now?" Alex whispered.

"Take it easy," I said, my own voice almost as panicky as his. "We'll get the boat loaded and let him park the car. He can do that much. Then we'll wait for Mom. Maybe you can talk him into taking a walk."

"Me? Why not you?"

I felt like saying: Hey I jumped in and saved Sid while you were trying to bean him with a life ring. "O.k. O.k. We'll both take him."

Dad backed the trailer down the ramp into the water.

Sid staggered to his feet and came over to help us load. He looked angry, scared, and sick. Dad pulled the boat back into the parking lot and got out to check the elastic tie-downs. "O.k. Let's go. It's getting late and I'm hungry."

"But, Dad, we've got to wait for Mom," I said.

"She can ride with that Marston guy. Come on."

I wanted one of the twins to handle this, but I was in charge. "Dad, if we're not here, Mom's gonna be really worried. Let's walk up the road to that grocery. You can buy a snack there."

He glared at me, then the boys. "You two, get in the car. Now."

They both looked at their feet. I saw Dad's face go chalky white and something in my gut set off an alarm. The doctors had warned us, and now it was about to happen. "Let's go," I said quietly.

We got in. Nobody said a word the whole twenty miles back into town. Dad hummed his tuneless hum, his big hands relaxed on the steering wheel. A big truck came up on our tail, then swung out and roared past with a blare of its air horn. I almost peed my pants as the wind blast shook the car, but Dad held the car straight with a flick of his wrist first one way and then the other.

I was counting the blocks home, when Dad turned off Aspen onto a side street. In the back, Alex let out a whine of pent-up fear. "Shut up," Sid whispered fiercely. "He's just taking the boat to the storage place."

We pulled up at the long row of rental garages in the low concrete building. "Get the keys, Shar," Dad said. I hopped out and ran to the office. Dad had the boat lined up with the metal door of our garage by the time I got back. He backed the boat in, and we unhitched the trailer. Dad stood for a long minute staring at the boat, and then ran a hand along the hull in a caress. "Smooth," he said. "Like glass."

We were eating leftover hot dish, the boys picking at it and Dad shoveling it away, when Mom opened the back door. I'd never seen her so mad. "Shar, get out here," she snapped. I went, closing the door behind me. Bob was standing in the garage with her, looking—for once—unsure of himself. "Shar, how could you let him do this? I nearly had a stroke when we saw you were gone."

"Mom, he—"

"My God, if he'd blacked out, you all could have been killed! I left you in charge and you let him—"

I started crying. "I didn't let him! He made us!"

"Made you? He couldn't make you. You had the keys."

"He found where I hid them. And if we hadn't done what he said, he would have left us there."

"Well, you should have stayed there and let him drive alone, instead of risking the lives of your brothers. Of all the irresponsible—"

I struck back. "Oh, sure, that's real easy for you to say! Where were you when Sid almost drowned and I had to save him because Alex couldn't think fast enough and Dad didn't care? Where the hell were you?" I was crying too hard to go on.

"Uh, Leslie," Bob said. "Maybe you ought to wait until—"

"And what's he doing here?" I glared at Mom. "Why's he got to stick his nose in our business?"

Mom took a step toward me, and I thought for a second that she was going to slap me. But instead she hugged me against her. "O.k., Shar. O.k. I'm sorry. I was just scared."

I felt her firm, athletic body under her business suit, breathed her elegant perfume, and I just couldn't stop crying. "And I'm fat and clumsy and Dad hates me and the boys won't listen to me. And Cindy's got Mark and I thought this other boy might call but he never did. And now you hate me and I just can't stand myself any longer."

She hugged me tighter. "Hush," she said. "Nobody hates you. Everything's o.k."

"No, it's not," I choked.

"Then it will be. Please stop crying, dear. Your mom's here, and I'm proud of you. You did the best you could. Just calm down and tell me what happened." I knew that she was almost crying too, but she's a lot stronger than I am.

Bob cleared his throat awkwardly. "Leslie, I think I should leave you two alone. Give me a call, huh?"

Mom nodded. "Thanks, Bob. Thanks for everything."

After he left, she did let herself cry a little as I told her what had happened on the lake. But they were classy, dab-the-eyes-a-little-bit tears. Then she gave me the ol' brave smile, patted my shoulder, and went to look at Sid's head. She decided that he ought to get checked for a concussion at the emergency room. Sid bitched, but she made him go with her.

Dad watched TV while Alex and I sat in the kitchen waiting. Alex fidgeted, then started doodling on a piece of paper—simple bunnies and flowers at first, but soon he was lost in drawing a complicated starship. "How can you do that at a time like this?" I groused.

He shrugged. "What do you want me to do?"

"You might worry a little."

"O.k., I'm worrying. Happy?"

I snorted and went to my room.

Sid came to my door, a thick bandage on the side of his head. "Are you o.k?" I asked.

"Ya, just a bruise. Heck, I've been hit harder playing football. How're your fingers?"

I took the ice pack off my hand and flexed them. "A little sore."

"I'm sorry. I guess that was my fault."

"No, it wasn't. Don't worry about it. They'll be o.k. in the morning."

He hesitated. "Uh, I wanted to say thanks for helping me this afternoon."

"You're welcome," I said. "You would have done the same for me."

"Ya, I guess. But I'm sorry I acted like such a baby."

"You weren't a baby. You'd just gotten clunked on the head with a ski. How were you supposed to act?"

He shrugged. "I don't know. Just better, I guess. How's Alex doing?"

"Oh, you know Alex. An earthquake could knock down the whole town and a half hour later he'd be just like always: 'Hey, guys, don't worry about it. Let's find something fun to do.'"

"Ya, that's Alex. Sometimes I think he's smarter than the rest of us. Anyway, thanks, Shar. I owe you one."

"No, you don't. I shouldn't have told you guys to get in the car. That was dumb. We should have let him leave without us."

"Maybe, but if you'd let him get real mad, he might have run into somebody."

"I never thought about anyone else. I was just scared

of him getting mad at us."

He hesitated, then shrugged again. "Well, the boat's stored away for the winter. We don't have to worry about waterskiing for a while."

I had a quick snack in the kitchen before going to bed. Mom and Dad were already in their bedroom. Pepper looked up from his rug in front of their door and wagged his tail. I tiptoed over to scratch his ears. "Do you need to go out, Pep?" I whispered. He put his head on his paws.

On the far side of the door, I could hear Dad talking. "The boys were real smooth. Sid took a couple of falls but he's better than Alex. And the boat ran good."

Mom didn't say anything for a moment, then asked— more to make conversation than anything, I guess— "How'd Shar do?"

Dad snorted. "She's a klutz. Doesn't even try. Next time I'm going to leave her home."

My eyes filled, and I spent a long moment with my face buried in Pepper's soft coat. He grunted, rolled onto his side, and thumped his tail. I gave his tummy a rub and, still trying not to cry, made my way quietly to the stairs.

Mom was off on another house-showing when I started making supper late Sunday afternoon. I turned from getting a can of green beans out of the pantry to find Dad blocking my way. He looked down at me with that strange stare. Slowly, his big hands came up to cover my breasts. I was so shocked that I went completely rigid. He squeezed them. "These are new," he said.

I tried to push his hands away. "No, dad. I've had them for a long time."

"I didn't see them before." He gave them another experimental squeeze, nothing suggestive but more like—I don't know—like he was squeezing a couple of oranges to see if they were fresh. Then he turned and walked away. I felt an acrid burning on the inside of my thigh and looked down to see a long stain running from my crotch to a puddle of urine on the floor between my shoes. I started crying as I grabbed for paper towels and Lysol. Oh, God, don't let the twins see me now.

Chapter 4

I changed my mind about telling Mom at least three dozen times in the next couple of days. Finally, I decided to let it go. I mean Dad hadn't felt me up like it was giving him a thrill or anything. It was more like he was just curious.

I remember an evening a couple of winters ago when Cindy and I were changing in the high school locker room before going to the pool for free swim. A woman near us had her little boy along and he pointed to us. "Mommy, how come those girls haven't got much hair down there?"

"Hush," she said. "They're not old enough."

"But you've got lots. And they only got—"

She was pretty sharp with him. "I said, hush. You're embarrassing them."

Cindy was giggling and blushing. I was just blushing. But there wasn't any real harm done. And that's sort of like it had been with Dad—just childish curiosity. Or at least that's what I wanted to believe.

Mark and Cindy had found love—or at least something close enough for her tastes. I wasn't liking her much these days, particularly when she expected me to listen to every detail about the great time they'd had Friday *and* Saturday nights. Mark told good jokes, he wasn't short of money, and "he dances divinely, daaar-ling."

"Oh, crap, Cindy," I said. "Spare me the old movie stuff, huh?"

"O.k. Oh, by the way, he kisses pretty good too."

"Lucky you," I said. "I hope he doesn't have that gum disease that's going around."

"What gum disease?"

"Oh, nothing much. Your teeth just fall out, that's all."

"You're kidding me, aren't you?" She actually sounded worried.

"Ya, I'm just kidding you."

We still walked to school together, but on the way home I was trailing farther and farther behind as Cindy and Mark walked hand-in-hand, giggling and looking soulfully into each other's eyes. In other words, acting generally disgusting. One of these days, I'd fade away completely. They'd never notice.

I was heading for the refrigerator on Wednesday night when the phone rang. I grumped a hello.

"Uh, Mrs. Zarada?"

"Just a second."

"No! Wait! Is this Shar?"

"Yes." Who the hey?

"This is Paul. You know, Paul O'Neil. I'm in biology with you."

I nearly dropped the phone. "*It is?* I mean, uh, hi, Paul. How are you?"

"Fine. Well, actually, I'm kind of nervous."

"Oh? Why?"

"Well, it seems like you've been avoiding me. So, I wasn't sure if I should take a chance on calling you. To ask if you're doing anything Friday night, that is. I mean, I'm sure you're going to be doing something, but I thought if you weren't real busy maybe you'd like to go—"

"Yes!"

"Uh, yes what?"

"Yes, I'll . . . What were you going to ask?"

"If you'd like to go to the movies. Say, are you as nervous as I am?"

"I think so. Maybe we ought to go back a little way."

"O.k. This is Paul O'Neil."

"Right. I got that part."

"Are you doing anything Friday night?"

"No." Keep it simple, Shar.

"Do you want to go to the movies?"

"Will I sound too eager if I say 'you bet'?"

"No, I think that'd be o.k. Early show or late?"

"Early."

"Do you want to go out for burgers before?"

"Sure," I said.

"Great. Shall I pick you up around six?"

"Sounds good."

He hesitated. "Have we covered everything? Wait. I think I'm supposed to ask when you've got to be home."

"I'll have to check. I haven't had a real date . . ." I almost said "before," but caught myself in time to say "in a while."

"O.k. So, I guess I'll see you tomorrow in school," he said.

"Right. I'll see you then."

We hung up. I don't know what he did then, but I just stood there for a stunned moment, then—holding it in—ran out the back door so I could let out a whoop and not get asked too many questions later.

Mom pulled out her pocket calendar. "Friday," she mused. "Here we are. Let's see." It had never crossed my mind that she might have something scheduled. Maybe I could make an excuse to Paul. Tell him that I'd had a heart attack or something, but that I'd be o.k. next week. Mom frowned at the page, then looked at me seriously, and my heart almost did stop. Then she grinned. "Well, I guess I can pass up the deal of the century so you can go to the movies."

"Really, Mom? You don't—"

"I was just teasing you, dear. I've got a showing at five, but I'll be home by six-thirty or seven. Just throw something on the table and let the boys clean up."

"Mind if I collapse on this chair in relief?"

"Go ahead. Now, do you need any motherly advice?"

"Uh, I don't think so."

"Want me to tell you about the birds and the bees and safe sex?"

"Mom, stop trying to embarrass me! We're just going to the movies."

She laughed. "Well, I'll help with your hair anyway." She headed for the living room, giving me a thump on the back as she passed. "And if he asks you to go out Saturday night, say yes. I'll be home." She did a little skip as she went through the door. How come she was so happy?

A couple of weeks before, I would have called Cindy right away with the news, but I decided to keep it to myself until the next morning when I could drop it off-hand on the way to school.

Cindy stared at me. "He did? Hey, that's great, Sharzar. Didn't I tell you he'd call?"

"Not exactly."

"Well, I told you he was interested, didn't I?"

"Ya, you were right as always, Cindy."

"Paul's a nice guy. Kind of quiet and he doesn't have a great bod, but—"

"How would you know?"

"Well, I don't really. I mean it looks like it's an o.k. bod, just—"

"Cindy, just let me enjoy this, huh? You can have your big sweaty guys."

"Mark isn't sweaty. Or even that big. What are you going to wear?"

"I haven't thought about it."

"Sharzar! You've got to start thinking about these things. I'd wear . . ." She prattled, and I tuned her out. A nice fall day. A *beautiful* fall day. You bet.

I planned to slip out the door the second I saw Paul coming up the driveway. That way the twins wouldn't have a chance to make any snide remarks. More important, Paul wouldn't have to meet Dad.

But then I got nervous and ran upstairs to check my hair a last time. I was trying to beat a runaway curl into submission when the doorbell rang and Pepper started barking furiously. Leave it to the stupid mutt to start acting like a watchdog for the first time in a year. I charged for the stairs, but I could already hear Sid opening the door. "Shar? There's no Shar here. . . . Oh, you mean Sharon. I'm not sure she's home. Alex, is Sharon home?"

"Hi, Paul," I said, as I hurried down the steps. I glared at Sid. Alex grinned at me from the next room, then made a face. "You know my kid brothers, Sid and Alex, don't you?"

"Ya, sure. I've seen you guys in the halls, haven't I?" He looked at me. "So, you ready to go?"

"Soon as I grab my jacket." I reached into the hall closet, and a shadow loomed over us. I turned to see Dad. He seemed bigger than ever tonight. Towering. "Oh, hi, Dad," I squeaked. "This is Paul."

Paul managed a smile. "Glad to meet you, Mr. Zarada."

Dad stared at Paul's outstretched hand, then shook it slowly. "Hi," he said.

"Dad, we've got to run. We're going to grab some burgers and then go to the movies." He nodded slowly, his stare fixed on Paul. Suddenly, I had a jolt of real fear. Dad had touched me, touched me where he shouldn't have. Maybe he did have a thing for his own daughter and now he'd see Paul as a rival. And he could squash Paul with one hand. Oh, please, Dad, don't do anything strange. "So," I said, "we'll see you later." Dad didn't move, just stared at us.

Sid said from the doorway, "Dad, the ball game's on." It seemed to take Dad a long second to understand that, but then he turned and followed Sid into the family room.

Neither one of us said anything until we were down the block a ways. "So," Paul asked, "do you prefer being called Sharon?"

"No, I hate it. That was just Sid teasing."

"Oh. Your brothers are in seventh, right?"

"Ya, the big time at last. Thank God I'll be in high school next year."

"I know what you mean. I had to walk my little sister to school and home every day until she was in fourth grade. I used to take a lot of crap about it. She's in fifth now."

"You're lucky she's not two years older."

"Ya, I guess things could be worse." He hesitated. "I don't think your dad liked me."

"Oh, he liked you o.k." Well, actually, he didn't like or not like you; he doesn't get into that kind of stuff anymore. "He's not feeling just right, that's all. He got real sick last spring. This artery in his brain swelled up and burst. He's still recovering and . . . Well, he's not quite with it yet."

"Oh. I'm sorry. . . . He's big, isn't he?"

"Ya, he is. So, you didn't even tell me what movie we're going to."

We managed to chat until we reached Hardee's. It was packed on a Friday night. We got our food just in time to grab a booth being vacated by a half dozen high school kids. Paul shoveled the leftover containers and cups onto a tray and took it to the wastebasket while I ran a couple of napkins over the table to soak up splattered ketchup and shake. He sat down, gesturing around the room and shouting over the noise. "I thought you'd like this better than Mac's. Quieter, more refined, you know."

I glanced around. "Ya, low lights, romantic atmosphere, strolling gypsy violinist. Who could ask for more?"

We laughed, and I think I took my first real look at him. He'd had a haircut and looked thoroughly scrubbed—not that he'd ever looked dirty or anything. "You look nice," I said.

"Thanks. So do you."

I guess I should learn to take compliments; I don't get enough to waste any. Instead, I stared at my reflection in the glass next to the booth. "Except my hair doesn't want to behave. God, I hate my curls."

"I like curly hair. The curlier the better. That's one of the first things I noticed about you this fall. Don't know why I didn't notice it before." He bent to take a bite of burger.

I stared at him. Paul, ol' buddy, you and I may get something going here. Heck, I'm half in love already. We held hands in the movie. Ya, I know, big thrill. But I liked it, even when my palm started sweating and he still didn't seem to want to let go. We had a soda afterward and walked around about two dozen extra blocks on the way home. I'd been praying for him to ask the right question—even hinting a couple of times that I didn't have any big plans for Saturday night. Instead, he said, "I'd like to take you out tomorrow night. I mean, if you don't have plans already, but I've got to baby-sit my sister."

"Oh. Too bad."

"But maybe we could do something tomorrow afternoon. Go roller-skating or something."

That almost spoiled it. I had visions of crashing to the rink and flopping there like a turtle on its back. Then Paul trying to help me up and me making him lose his balance and— "Uh, I've got kind of weak ankles. Could we do something else?"

"Oh, sure. Hey, would you like to make a pizza over at my house? I could rent a videotape too. We'd have to put up with my little sister some of the time, but maybe I could bribe her into going to bed early."

"I'll make brownies for dessert. Do you like brownies?"

"Does a bear . . . Uh, you know."

"Poop in the woods," I said.

"Close enough." He grinned. "Just bring the mix.

We'll put Jilly to work stirring it. That'll keep her out of the way."

Cindy called before I'd even pried my eyes open on Saturday morning. "How'd it go?"

I yawned. "Fine. He's fun."

"Did he ask you out for tonight?"

"He's got to baby-sit, but I'm going over to his house. We're going to make pizza."

"Mark's going to take me to the dance in Hartlin. We're doubling with a friend of his who's got a license and a car."

"Have a good time."

"Jeez, it's too bad that Paul's got to baby-sit or you guys could come too. I mean baby-sitting and making pizza sounds kind of boring when your best friend—"

I cut her off, surprised at the sharpness in my voice. "Cindy, I really don't want to get into any kind of competition thing here. Have a great time. So will we. Or at least we're going to try."

"Ya, sure. I didn't mean anything. I just wish you guys were coming along. . . . So, do you want to go downtown this morning?"

"I can't. Mom said we've got to do the yard today."

"Oh. Well, maybe I'll see you tomorrow."

"O.k. Hey, Cindy, I'm sorry if I sounded bitchy. You have a really great time."

"Ya, you too."

"And, Cindy, remember me telling you that I was kidding about that gum disease?"

"Yes?"

"I lied."

"Sharzar!" she screamed. I hung up the phone and grinned.

66

I got dressed, my brain starting to click over at something approaching normal speed. God, I felt great. I pulled my nightie over my head and paused for a moment to look at myself in the full-length mirror. Not too bad—if I could just do something about this gut. Starting today, I would. Low-cal all the way, girl.

Sid kicked the lawn mower. "Damn mower. Now what's wrong?"

Alex edged him aside. "Kicking it isn't going to help." He crouched by the mower, studying the engine. "Dad used to clean the spark plug, didn't he?"

Sid stared at Dad sitting on a lawn chair, gazing at the portable TV on the picnic table, and dipping into his big bowl of snacks. "Ya, he used to clean the plug and set the gap or something. Why can't the big baby do it now? Last weekend he got the outboard running, but what's he doing today? Just sitting there getting fat."

I felt like telling him to shut up, but I was in too good a mood to fight with Sid. "I think the instruction manual is above the workbench. And maybe a new plug."

"Sounds like what we need," Alex said. He strolled toward the garage.

Sid looked after him irritably. "Well, don't hurry, Alex. We've got all day to waste on this stupid yard." He came over, picked up a pair of shears, and started hacking at a bush.

"Don't do that," I said. "I just finished that one."

"Not short enough," he growled. "We ought to cut these things right down to the ground." But he stopped hacking and began picking up branches. "God, I hate yard work."

"You're not the only one," I sympathized, even though I actually kind of enjoyed it. I got off the ladder, wiped the sweat from my forehead, and reached for my safety glasses and the electric trimmer. Alex was back at the lawn mower, carefully loosening the plug with a socket wrench.

"Shar." Sid's voice had changed. He pointed to the far gate hanging open on its hinges. Dad's chair was empty.

"Oh, crap," I heard myself say. I dropped the trimmer and hurried after him.

He was walking steadily down the block toward the nature preserve, Pepper trotting at his side. I broke into a jog to catch up. Pepper heard me coming and thought I wanted to play. He took off, making a wide circle through a vacant lot, then shooting by me with a quick nip at my heels. "Not now, Dumbo," I said. I caught up to Dad. "Where are you going, Dad?"

"Down to the lake. I saw some ducks go over. I want to see if they're down there."

I'd seen them too. Every year, thousands of them fly in to the marshy area west of town to rest up before starting the long flight south. "Dad, I wish you'd tell us when you're going somewhere. You know, in case you get a call or something."

"Nobody calls me. They haven't since I got sick last spring."

"Well, you can never tell. Uh, besides, maybe one of us would like to go with you."

"Why?"

"I don't know. Just to be with our dad." He grunted.

I had to hurry to keep up as we cleared the last row of houses and started down the long slope into the nature preserve. Through the trees, the lake glittered in the afternoon sun. Dad stopped and squinted for a long moment. "No ducks," he said. "No geese either." He turned on his heel and started for home.

Pepper snuffled in some tall grass, then came bounding toward us. I hadn't seen him so energetic in I couldn't remember when. Dad watched him. "Maybe we ought to go after some ducks this fall, dog. What'd you think of that? I'll shoot 'em, you swim out and get 'em. Sound good?" Pepper wagged his tail and grinned. That just about took the last of my breath away. Hunting? Dad couldn't hunt again. Not this fall, not ever. Oh, God, Mom, why can't you be home more?

Alex had the lawn mower going and Sid was trimming when we got back. Dad didn't go to his seat by the picnic table but disappeared into the house. Twenty minutes later, I went in to check on him. He was sitting in the den, the pieces of his long, double-barreled shotgun laid out on the bed. He looked up, irritation on his face. "Ya?"

"Uh, Dad, maybe you ought to put some newspaper or plastic under those parts. You know, to keep oil from getting on the bedspread."

He looked down, studying the problem. "Get some."

I hate guns. I tried to tell myself that it was o.k. to leave Dad and the twins alone and go to Paul's. After all, Mom had locked up all the ammunition, and Dad was no homicidal maniac or anything. Just a sick guy who couldn't feel a lot of things anymore. But I couldn't talk myself into leaving him alone with the boys. I called Paul and told him that I'd be late.

"Jilly and I were going to walk over and pick you up."

"I can find your place. Why don't you start the dough or something? I'll get there as soon as I can."

"O.k. Say, there's no problem, is there?"

"No," I lied. "Uh, one of the twins doesn't feel just right, that's all. I think I'd better stick around until Mom gets home."

I put supper on the table, and Dad and the boys ate while I watched the clock. When Mom finally pulled into the driveway, I went out to tell her about the shotgun. Mom doesn't like guns either, and she went a little white. She took a deep breath. "Do the boys know?"

"I don't think so. He was done cleaning the gun when we came in."

"Well, let's not tell them right now. Maybe he'll forget about it."

"Mom, you're not going to let him go hunting, are you?"

"No, of course not." She forced herself to sound cheerful. "Now you've got a big date. We'll worry about everything else later. Want me to give you a ride over?"

I glanced at my watch. "No, go eat. It's only a few blocks."

"Call when you want me to pick you up."

"I can walk home."

"No, I don't want you walking by yourself after dark."

"Oh, Mom. This is New Bremen not some big city."

"That doesn't matter. Want me to ground you right now?"

"Tyrant," I said, and she laughed.

It wasn't until I was halfway to Paul's that I remembered that I hadn't taken time to shower or change clothes. Darn it, Shar, you've already let your figure go, is personal hygiene next? I sniffed an armpit suspiciously. I was still all right. But I was going to have to start remembering things, instead of spending all my time worrying about Dad and what he might or might not do.

We had a really good time. The pizza turned out better than the ones Cindy and I made. Paul's sister was a

70

nice kid, even though she did give a disgusted snort when Paul took my hand during the videotape. I'd worried a little that it might be a movie with a lot of heavy sex. In the theater you can blush and nobody notices, but in Paul's living room I wasn't sure how I was going to handle it. But he'd picked a family thing about some mountain man making friends with lots of animals. It was a little short on excitement but pretty.

I called Mom after the movie was over and Paul was forcing Jilly to go to bed. Mom said, "It's a beautiful evening. I think I'll walk over."

"Aren't you worried about walking alone after dark?"

"Don't get snippy. I'll see you in a few minutes."

Paul came into the kitchen. "So, I'm glad you came."

"So am I."

"Is it too early to get in a reservation for next weekend?"

"I don't think so."

"Good." He shuffled. "Want to wait on the steps until your mom comes?"

"O.k."

We sat under the moon in the autumn night. *Ro-mantic,* let me tell ya. Paul had his arm around me, and I knew that he was trying to get up the courage to kiss me. I sent a couple of encouraging brain waves his way, but he almost waited too long anyway. We saw Mom pass under the streetlight down the block. Paul took a quick breath and pulled me toward him. And I moved a little too fast his way. Our lips didn't exactly meet, and he mostly got my upper lip. (Thank God I didn't have a runny nose or anything.) It was over in about half a second, and I'd been kissed for the first time. That's if you didn't count some dumb games in grade school.

We looked at each other for a confused few seconds,

71

then giggled. "Uh, I guess I need some practice," Paul said.

"That's o.k.," I said. "I'm glad you're not an expert." I glanced down the block quickly, then gave his hand a squeeze, and moved a little away.

Mom came to the fence. "O.k., break it up in there," she called.

"That's just Mom's sense of humor," I said. "Ignore her. I'll see you Monday. Maybe you can walk me home from school."

"That'd be great."

"You bet," I said.

Mom wasn't in any hurry, and we strolled along enjoying the night. "Well," she said, "did you get a kiss good-night?"

"Mom! You're not supposed to ask things like that."

"Oh, yes I am. What do you think mothers are for?" She gave me a nudge. "Come on, you can tell me."

"No, I can't."

"Want me to suspect the worst?"

"O.k., o.k. I did, but, well. . . . He kinda missed. I mean not completely, but he wasn't dead on."

Mom laughed. "That's normal. It usually doesn't work so well the first time."

"What happened to you?"

"I'm not telling."

"Mom, you'd better!"

"Oh, o.k." She giggled. "He let me go so fast that I fell off the steps. Plop. Right in two feet of snow."

"You didn't!" I laughed. "What did you do?"

"The only thing I could. I made an angel."

We both started laughing hard, holding onto each other and trying to walk at the same time—the way

Cindy and I did sometimes. "And what'd he do?" I choked.

"He stood there kind of stunned for a moment and then he jumped in and made an angel too. We got snow all down our backs."

"Who was it, Mom?"

She hesitated a long moment, then said quietly, "Your father."

"Dad? He wasn't the first guy you ever kissed, was he?"

"Not exactly. But he was the first one who mattered." She looked at me carefully in the dim light. "Was Paul?"

I shrugged. "Well, not exactly, but the others don't seem to count right now. It was just playground and party stuff, you know. Like do you dare to trade a few germs to see what it's like."

She smiled. "Yes, I know." She put an arm around my shoulders for a moment. "Just take it easy and enjoy yourself."

Oh, oh, I thought. Here comes the lecture. But she didn't say anything, and when I took a quick look at her, she was smiling kind of dreamily to herself. "Mom, why the heck are you so happy tonight? I thought parents were supposed to get real uptight when their kids started dating."

She shrugged. "Oh, I trust you to know right from wrong." She gave me another nudge. "Or smart from dumb anyway."

"Ya, but what's with this happy-talk number?"

"I'm just happy for you, dear. It hasn't been an easy six months. Now you've got a chance to have a little fun. That makes me happy." She looked at me seriously. "Just don't spoil it by worrying too much. Relax."

"Ya, like you're always so relaxed?"

"That's different. I'm an adult. I've earned the right to screw-up my head."

"Right." I said sarcastically.

We walked for a block without saying anything. Mom started humming some sappy love song from the Sixties. Passing under a streetlight, I glanced at her again. She still had that funny half-smile on her face. And suddenly an icy feeling hit me square in the gut. Wait a second. I don't buy all this dreamy crap. You're not thinking about me and Paul, or you and Dad, or you and some other guy you knew a long time ago. You're thinking about somebody you know right now. And I know who.

I almost told her that right then and there. But, darn it, this was my night. I wouldn't let her spoil it. Not her or anybody. But I guess I did a pretty good job of that on my own.

Chapter 5

Shar XXX Paul. I wanted to paint it in big letters on the railroad viaduct over the highway. Or go down to the lake and carve it inside a valentine's heart on the biggest tree around. Or take out a loan and buy a full-page ad in the newspaper. Or . . .

Two dates and one fumbled kiss, and I'd gone completely over the edge. What made it even crazier was that I'd seen Paul around junior high every day for two years, but I couldn't recall ever giving him a second glance, much less fantasizing about having him for a boyfriend. Then, *alla-ka-wham,* he was just about the most wonderful thing that'd ever happened to me. Just crazy. But skeptical, down-to-earth Shar Zarada would be darned if she was going to pause long enough to talk any sense to herself.

Monday morning he was waiting by my locker when I got to school. After school we walked home together, trailing Mark and Cindy by a few feet, then a few dozen, then half a block. The next day we didn't even bother to meet them outside the main doors but went our own way. He took me out both nights the next weekend. We practiced our kissing some on Friday and really got the hang of it on Saturday. Definitely.

I caught myself looking in my mirror a lot, trying to

figure out what he could see in me. I smiled seductively at my image, bounced on my tiptoes to see if I bounced at all in the right places, and tried sashaying away while giving a come-hither look over my shoulder. The last one didn't work so hot, because my butt always looked gigantic, so I worked mostly on my front poses. Maybe I'd have to ask him for a picture to stick on the frame of my mirror so I could really get in the spirit. But how about when I didn't have any clothes on? I mean, I couldn't have his picture just staring at me then, could I? Or maybe that was part of the fun. God, there were a lot of things to figure out about this boyfriend stuff.

I got out of the shower on Wednesday morning and toweled every last gram of water off my skin before stepping on the scale. O.k., think light. I looked down. Only a pound? No, it had to be more; I'd been starving myself for more than a week. I jiggled the scale and looked again. Pound and a half? Ya, call it a pound and a half. A start anyway.

I wrapped a towel around me and scurried for my room, my mind on what I should wear. I let out a yip of surprise at the door; Dad was standing at my window watching the sky. "Dad! What are you doing?"

"Looking for geese," he said, not turning.

"Oh." I pulled the towel a little higher and held on to the sides so it wouldn't flap. "Did you see any?"

"No."

I waited, but he didn't seem about to move. "Dad, I've got to get ready for school now. Could I have a little privacy?" He gave me an irritated look, then started for the door. I moved aside to let him pass. Let's see, maybe I ought to wear my new blue sweater. It's maybe a little warm, but—

Dad stopped in the doorway and stared me up and down. I had a jolt of fear. Oh, my God. I took a couple of steps back, hugging the towel tightly across my chest. "Dad, please go. Please don't—"

"You're short," he said. "You've always been short but when did you get so fat?" He kept staring at me. "Well?"

"I . . . I don't know, Dad. Last winter, I guess. I'm . . . I'm on a diet now." He grunted and walked out.

I wouldn't cry! Not when Paul would see my red eyes the second I got to school. I pulled on the first clothes I found, grabbed my books, and beat it out the front door. "Hey, Shar," Alex called from the kitchen. "Aren't you going to eat breakfast?" I let the closing door give my answer. Choking down the big lump in my throat, I headed for Cindy's.

At her door, I knocked once and walked in. She was just finishing breakfast. "Sharzar! Is something the matter?"

"No. I just thought I'd pick you up for a change."

"Oh. . . . How come your hair's still wet?"

"I thought you could help me with it. We've got a few minutes."

"Well, o.k., I guess." She looked skeptical.

In her bathroom, she ladled on a half-gallon of mousse and went after my curls with a hair dryer and a brush. "Maybe you ought to try some of that straightening stuff," she said.

"Paul likes curly hair."

"Maybe so, but there's curly and there's ridiculous. Get down there." She whacked a curl with the brush.

"Ouch," I said.

"Sorry, I forgot there was somebody under there." For a long minute, she didn't say anything. "So, what's the matter, Sharzar?"

"I told you, nothing."

"Bull. Did you and Paul have a fight or something?"

"No, we're fine." And despite all my determination, I started crying.

"What? Does he want more than you're willing to give right now? Sex, you know."

"No. We're fine, really. It's Dad. He's . . ." I felt her hands hesitate, then she made a noncommittal sound, and went on brushing. I snuffled back tears and daubed at my eyes. "He's just gotten more difficult recently."

"Oh. I'm sorry."

"You don't want to hear the details."

"You can tell me if it helps. But, Sharzar—" She glanced at the clock on the wall. "Maybe we ought to save it for later."

"Sure," I said, and wiped my nose again.

She sighed. "Sharzar, I do care. Really. It's just, well, you just can't let it get to you all the time. You've got to keep going." I nodded, and she patted me on the shoulder. "Now let me get you some eye drops. We'll talk about something happy on the way to school."

I wasn't worth a darn all day. It was all I could do to keep from crying every time I thought about Dad. Before he got sick, he'd never said anything cruel to me or touched me where I shouldn't. And I'd never been afraid of him.

I kept remembering scenes from when we were buddies, and he never criticized me for being clumsy or plump or just not perfect. Like the morning when I was maybe nine and we'd gone fishing together—just the two of us. We walked down to the lake and sat on the long dock that stretched out from the shore over water so still and clear that you could see fish swimming five or six feet down. Dad opened his Thermos of coffee and poured himself a cup, then started getting our rods ready. He handed one to me and then popped the top off the plastic container of night crawlers. "Want me to put the worm on, or do you want to do it yourself?" I'd never liked handling worms, and he knew it. But I was ashamed not to, now that the boys had learned how. "I'll bait my own hook," I said a little huffily. He smiled slightly, handed me a night crawler, then set about baiting his hook.

My crawler wasn't enthusiastic about getting poked with a hook. I couldn't blame him, but I didn't sympathize a darn bit either. I was so mad by the time I finally got the slimy little monster balled up that I jammed the hook in extra hard—straight through his body and into the ball of my thumb.

I was yelping and bouncing up and down when Dad's big hand went around my wrist. "Stop jumping around, Shar. You're just driving it in farther." He put his other hand on my shoulder and squeezed hard. I stopped bouncing. "Shar, your daddy's here. But you've got to sit still so I can fix things. Can you do that?"

I nodded through tears, and he released the pressure on my shoulder and turned to dig in his tackle box. "But it hurts, Daddy."

"I know. Just hold on."

"What are you going to do?"

"Well, first I'm going to try to save that night crawler. They're too expensive to throw away these days."

"Daddy!"

He found the pliers and turned back to me, that gentle smile on his face. "Do you think I ought to throw him away?"

"Put him someplace where I can squish him!"

He laughed, then leaned over my hand. I was still crying some, but he was squeezing my wrist so hard that I could barely feel any part of my hand. "Well, maybe we'll just toss ol' Mr. Crawler in the lake. Let the fish have something for free." He clipped away the line and the crawler, and examined my thumb. He whistled a few notes through his teeth. "Well, daughter, you did it like a true Zarada."

I tried to get a look. "What do you mean?"

"You hooked it good, that's all. Don't wiggle." He put down the pliers, and slipped a jackknife from his pocket, snapping open the blade with that quick little flick of the thumb that the boys always tried to imitate but could never get.

"What are you going to do?" I said in real alarm.

He leaned over my hand. "Just cutting a little bit of skin so the barb will come out easier. Now relax. Want me to tell you a story?"

"No."

"That's too bad; I've got the perfect one for the situation. Look real close at the back of my left ear. Do you see a scar?"

I looked. "Kind of a white spot?"

"That's it. Now look real careful at my scalp next to it. You should see two more."

I looked. "What happened?"

He set down the knife and picked up the pliers again. "I was casting for muskie up on the Chippewa Flowage from that old aluminum fishing boat we used to have. I'd had this big muskie on early in the afternoon but lost him right next to the boat. All afternoon I tried to hook him again but didn't get a nibble—"

"Were the boys along?"

"No, this was before they were born."

"Was I born yet?"

"Yes, but you were real little. Too little to go fishing. Now let me tell the story."

"O.k."

"Anyway, when it started getting on toward dark, I figured Mr. Muskie had beaten me. But I decided to give him one last chance before heading in. So I hauled back and really let the ol' bait fly." He laughed. "And I caught my head instead of the fish. One prong of the treblehook in the ear, two in the scalp. Hurt like a son of a gun."

He paused for a second, and I could feel him start to work the hook loose from my thumb. "I knew that there was nothing I could do about it out in the middle of the lake, so after I got done swearing, I clipped the line and drove back to shore. I put my tackle in the car and loaded my boat. There were some other fishermen around, and they stared a bit at that big bait just dangling from my head like a big earring. But I didn't say anything, just made like I always wore it."

In spite of myself, I started giggling. He grinned. "Hold still just a minute more." He picked up the knife again. "So, I drove into town, asked at a bar where the nearest doctor lived, and drove over to his place. He was this little old guy with an office right in his home. He saw me and started laughing. Then he says in this gravelly voice, 'Well, I hope you got your limit first, young fella. Come on in and I'll relieve you of that souvenir.' He told me that he'd take it out for five bucks if he could keep the bait. I said that was o.k. by me, as long as he didn't keep my ear too. So he unhooked me and then he showed me his den. I'll bet you he had nearly a hundred baits hanging on the wall. All out of fishermen's ears and scalps. . . . There." He leaned back and held up the hook. "And I'm going to keep this one for the wall of my den."

He let me have my hand back, and I looked at my thumb. After all the work he'd done, there was only a tiny cut. He dug a can of first-aid spray and a bandage out of his tackle box. "Think you'll live?" he asked.

"I guess."

He sprayed and bandaged my thumb, then leaned over to give it a kiss. "Add a big kiss and it'll be good as new."

I pulled my hand away. "Dad, I'm not a little girl anymore."

He grinned, his blue eyes twinkling. "As long as I'm your daddy, you'll always be my little girl." He threw a big arm around me and hugged me to his side, his other hand knuckling my scalp. "And there ain't nothin' you can do about it! Now admit it or I'll throw you in the lake."

I was laughing. "O.k., o.k. I'm still your little girl."

He let me go. "That's better. Now shall we see if there are any fish in this lake?"

"O.k., but can you bait my hook this time?"

"My pleasure. Just remember where the pliers are in case I stick myself."

That was the way it used to be. On that day and a thousand others. Back when I was still his little girl and thought I always would be.

I fought off the blues. I didn't want to lay my problems on Paul and spoil what we had. He was sweet, sticking little notes through the vent in my locker when we couldn't meet between classes. The notes didn't say a whole lot, and he made only one attempt at poetry, but he was thinking about me. And I was sure thinking about him, as I counted the hours until the weekend.

He was impatient too and asked me if I could go out Wednesday night. I wasn't surprised when Mom squashed that one: "Nope. Dating is for the weekends."

"But, Mom, Cindy and some of the other girls get to go out during the week. I mean, not real late and not real often, but—"

"That's up to their parents. I say no, not until you're older."

"How much older?"

"Thirty-five maybe."

"Thirty-five! That's almost as old as you are."

"Don't I wish," she said. "And if you start mentioning that I'm about to turn forty, you can start spending Fridays and Saturdays at home."

"My having a boyfriend gives you a lot of new power, doesn't it?"

She grinned. "Figured that one out, huh?"

Friday night, Paul and I went to the football game at the high school. It was great, even though I don't give a darn about football. We snuggled together under a blanket and held hands except when we had to jump up to cheer with the rest of the crowd. Neither of us was paying much attention to the game, but it seemed the thing to do and jumping around kept the circulation going in the legs.

Afterward, we had the long walk across town to our neighborhood with quite a few pauses along the way to practice our kissing. We were getting real good at it. A block from my house, he asked, "Can you still come over to watch a videotape tomorrow night?"

"I'm counting on it."

"Great. Hey, I'm sorry I've got to baby-sit again, but it's about the easiest money I can make."

"I understand. Your parents are going out at eight, right?"

"Right. Would you believe a Fifties party? Dad said he's going to comb his hair in a ducktail. I'll believe that when I see it."

I hesitated, not sure if he'd like my idea. "Mom wants me to ask you over for a picnic in the backyard. I guess she wants to check you out."

"Worried that I'm going to corrupt you?"

"Are you? I was kind of hoping."

"Well, I'm willing to try, but I think it's kind of like kissing. You know, it takes some practice."

"As long as you're practicing on me." I pulled him into the shadow of a hedge and laid a good one on him.

"I think it's my mom who ought to worry about you," he said after a minute.

"We'll worry about one mom at a time. So is it o.k? You wouldn't mind coming for a picnic before we go over to your house?"

"No, it'll be fun. What time?"

Mom made the hamburger patties in the kitchen, while I got the gas grill going out back. Dad and the twins were playing catch, nothing fancy today, just lazily throwing the ball around. Alex said, "I've gotta go to the bathroom. Shar, do you want to take my place?"

I was too nervous to stand around just watching the grill and waiting for Paul, so I said, "Sure." He tossed me his glove, and I took the corner nearest the fence. I was even klutzier than usual. I kept missing and having to scamper after the ball. About the third time I dug it out from under a bush, I turned to find Dad staring darkly at me. I tried to grin. "Don't worry. I'll get the hang of it." I tossed the ball to Sid, who pegged it to Dad. But instead of throwing it on to me, Dad fired it back to Sid, nearly catching him looking the other way.

Sid glanced my way and hesitated. "Don't throw it to her," Dad snapped. "She'll just miss." Sid shrugged and threw it to Dad.

Alex came out of the house and ambled over to where I was watching Dad and Sid play. "What happened?" he asked.

"Never mind," I said, and handed him the glove.

Paul came to the fence a few minutes later, and I ran to open the gate. "Hi," I said. "You're late."

He glanced at his watch. "Am I? Not according to my watch."

"Your watch is two minutes slow. Come on, Mom should have the hamburgers ready for the grill."

In the garage on the way to the back door, I pulled him into a corner out of sight of the backyard and laid a fast kiss on him. "Gosh, I'm glad to see you."

He grinned, looking both pleased and a little embarrassed. "Thanks. Me too."

His arms came out for me, but I put my hands on his chest. "That's all for now; we might get caught."

"Right," he said. "Besides, I'm hungry."

"You're always hungry. How come you don't weigh five hundred pounds? I would if I ate like you, and I already weigh too much."

"I think you're just right," he said. (Any wonder that I loved the guy?)

The phone rang just as we came into the kitchen.

Mom gave us a smile and a little wave as she answered it. "Hello. Oh, hello, Bob." She pointed to the platter of hamburger patties.

We got the hamburgers on the grill. Pepper was lurking in the shade under the picnic table, hoping for an accident. "Stay away from the burgers, Dumbo," I told him. "Or we'll have roast dogmeat."

"Would that be putting on the dog?" Paul said.

"You're sick," I said. "Come on, let's get the rest of the food."

Mom was still on the phone, listening with a serious expression. We'd finished setting the table before she came out. She glanced with irritation at Dad and the twins still playing catch. "Didn't the boys help at all?"

"It's o.k., Mom. We've got everything under control."

"Well, they should help when we've got a guest." She checked the underside of one of the hamburgers, then sat down at the table and crunched a celery stick. "Rats, we lost the buyer on that white elephant in the country. Double rats." She sighed. "Well, you don't want to listen to me complain. How's school going, Paul?"

"Fine, Mrs. Zarada."

"Good. So, Shar tells me you like building models. My boys like that too."

Paul looked embarrassed about being compared to a couple of twelve-year-olds. "Well, they're not what you usually think of as models, Mrs. Zarada. A couple of friends and I build bridges out of toothpicks. Then we see how much weight it takes to crush them. There's a national contest every year, and we're going to enter when we find the best design. You, uh, go through a lot of glue and toothpicks."

"Mom, I think the hamburgers are done," I said.

She got up for a look, turned the gas low, then called, "Ken, Sid, Alex, come and eat." The boys started for the table, but Dad said, "In a few minutes. We're just warmed up."

Mom's lips tightened, but then she gave us a smile. "Well, let them play a few more minutes. You guys get first choice of burgers." The three of us filled our plates. Mom turned to Dad and the twins again. "Come on before the burgers dry out." Dad ignored her, and the twins looked at her helplessly.

I thought later that she should have gone over to talk to Dad. But instead she glared at the boys and made a short angry gesture at the food on the table. They started our way.

"Sid!" Dad snarled. Sid reacted just in time to keep the ball from taking his head off. "You'll stop playing when I tell you to stop playing!"

The rest of us stared at them. Mom opened her mouth, but Sid cut her off. "It's o.k., Mom. I'm not hungry anyway." He fired the ball back at Dad.

Mom tried her best to recover, and Paul tried his best to make like he hadn't seen a thing. Alex gave me a well-what-can-you-really-do shrug and loaded his plate. Sid and Dad kept playing catch. Each time Dad threw, Sid pegged it back harder. Dad grinned like a wolf. Mom had her back to them, but I could tell that she heard the faster and faster crack of the ball hitting the gloves. When Sid finally missed one and the ball came ricocheting past the grill, she spun. "Sid, Ken, that's enough! Now come and eat."

Sid dropped his glove without a glance at Dad and walked over to the table. He grabbed a plate and went to the grill. Dad stood glaring after him. Alex said, "Hey,

Paul, did you and Jim Phelps make that toothpick bridge in the science room?"

"Ya. Jim, me, and Tom Woodward."

"That's a really neat bridge. What kind of glue did you use?"

After a long minute, Dad came to the table. Mom got him a hamburger. "There you are, dear. Just tell me if you want another." She took her place again and did her best to smile at the rest of us. "Well, Paul, what movie did you rent for—"

Dad spun and smashed his plate to the ground. "When I want to play ball, I want to play ball! Not sit around with a bunch of wimps!" He jumped to his feet so fast that his lawn chair toppled. He stumbled over it, nearly fell, then snatched it off the grass and hurled it halfway across the yard. He stood glaring at us, his chest heaving and his hands working like he wanted to throttle someone. Instead, he grabbed his glass and fired it against the side of the house where it exploded in a shower of glass and red Kool-Aid. Then he was off marching across the yard toward the gate, the street, the edge of town, and the lake beyond.

We sat in stunned silence. Under the table, Pepper whined uncertainly, then wiggled out past me and trotted after Dad. Mom took her napkin from her lap, put it carefully beside her plate, then reached across the table to touch Paul's arm. "I'm sorry, Paul. Mr. Zarada is not himself just now. You'll have to forgive him—and me too." She looked at me. "Shar, you and Paul go ahead and have your date. Boys, finish eating, then clean up. Now please excuse me." She got up and walked toward the gate still swinging on its hinges. I could tell by the set of her shoulders that she was trying hard not to cry. And, God, how I hated her. And Dad.

* * *

We walked in the opposite direction. Paul had his hands in his pockets, and he didn't look at me. "Well," he said at last, "I guess it wasn't such a good idea for me to come."

I started crying. "I'm sorry. God, I'm so sorry."

"Hey, it's o.k. Don't cry, huh?" We stood on the sidewalk, me crying and him standing there with his hands in his pockets—just when I wanted very much for him to put his arms around me. At last, he said, "Uh, I think maybe we should start walking before your neighbors start wondering."

I didn't give a darn what the neighbors thought, but I started walking anyway, my eyes so blurry that I could hardly see the sidewalk. Somehow I had to make him understand that Dad wasn't really a monster, that it wasn't Dad's fault that his brain didn't work right anymore. I tried very hard but nothing I said came out very clearly, because I was crying like I'd wanted to cry all the months since Dad had fallen off the forklift.

Paul didn't say much, just walked beside me, his hands still in his stupid pockets. It was nearly dark when we stopped in front of his house. He glanced at his watch, then uncertainly at the front door. "I've got to go in." He hesitated. "I don't imagine you feel much like a movie tonight." I shook my head. "Are you going to be o.k? I mean, maybe Mom and Dad could drop you at home on their way to the party."

"I want to walk. I'll be o.k."

"Well, I guess I'll see you Monday then."

"Paul, I'm really sorry. Dad's just . . . just a little crazy sometimes. He didn't mean any of that junk about wimps and stuff."

Paul shrugged. "I'm not holding anything against anybody. The whole thing was . . . I don't know, kind of surprising, I guess."

We stood for a moment. "Can you just forget about tonight?" I asked.

"Sure. No sweat. Uh, you take care, huh?"

I grabbed him before he could turn away and gave him a quick, hard kiss, then hurried away so he didn't see me starting to cry all over again.

In the garage, the twins were shadows against the dim light coming through the door to the backyard. Mom sat at the picnic table, Pepper almost invisible beside her. Dad stood in the middle of the yard, tossing the baseball into the night sky. "How long have they been home?" I whispered.

"About half an hour," Alex whispered back. "He's pretty calm now, and Mom's trying to talk to him. She wants him to apologize to you, but he doesn't seem to get it. He said Paul's—"

"Shut up," Sid said. "She doesn't need to hear that."

"Well," Alex said, "he called us all wimps. What's the difference if he called Paul one too?"

"Did I ever mention that you've got crap for brains?" Sid said. "Now, shut up and listen."

Dad flipped the ball into the air and caught it again. Then he started talking, his voice soft and strange. "I can feel the ball whiz from my hands. Feel the spiral. And I like to watch the boys catch it. Not because they're my sons, but because they're good at it. It's almost like watching a game on TV. Balance, talent, I can still understand those things. I lost all that for a while, but I got it back. I can't feel most things that people are supposed to feel, but at least I got that little bit of something back." Suddenly, his voice turned angry. "But Shar can't catch worth a damn and it hurts to watch her! So, she's not playing with us anymore."

"Ken, it's not playing catch that matters. It's keeping control of your temper. Now that boy Paul is a nice kid, and he's good for Shar. You've got to—"

The ball fell at Dad's feet and he stood unmoving, his turned-up face flattened almost featureless by the pale light of the moon. I heard Mom's sharp intake of breath. She sat for a moment, then got up and went to him. She picked up the ball and put it in his outstretched glove, then returned to her seat and waited for him to come back from wherever the blackout had taken him in that starry sky.

I turned away and went into the house. Alex caught me at the stairs. "Hey, Shar, I'll still play catch with you."

I shook my head and plodded up the steps, too tired to cry any more that night.

A long time later, I felt Mom slip into my bed and put an arm around me. "I'm sorry, Shar," she whispered, and started crying very softly against my curls. I loved her very much then and turned over to get my arms around her. I think for a moment in my drowsiness I understood something about women sticking together because we had to or none of us could take it. And, for that little while, everything was o.k. because I knew that somehow we'd make it no matter what happened.

Chapter 6

"Hey, Shar, wake up!"

I turned over and pried my eyes open to see Alex at the door. "Why? What's the matter?"

"It's Dad. He's gone."

"Where? When?" I rolled out of bed and reached for my bathrobe.

"We don't know. When Mom woke up, he was just gone. The car's gone too."

Mom was on the phone in the kitchen. This time she didn't look calm and efficient but scared. Real scared. "Yes. . . . All right." She nodded as if the person on the other end could see her. "I know. Thanks, Bob. We'll see you in a few minutes." She hung up and turned to look at the three of us. "Do any of you have any idea. . . ?" She let the question trail off. We shook our heads.

I don't know how she can keep it together sometimes, but she always seems to. She took a ragged breath, willing calm back into the room. "Well, get some breakfast," she said. "I'm going to get my clothes on and comb my hair before Bob gets here. We'll find your dad."

"Mom, maybe we should call the police," I said.

"He's not done anything wrong, Shar. For all we know, he's just taking a drive in his own car."

She hurried out before I could argue. The three of us looked at each other. Sid said, "He's getting worse. A lot worse. One of these days something really bad is going to happen."

I tried to do my best Mom imitation. "Well, going hungry isn't going to make anything any better." I retied my bathrobe and started for the pantry. "Do you guys want pan—" A thought hit me, and I turned to look quickly around the room. "Hey, where's Pepper? Has anyone seen him?"

Sid said, "Oh, who cares about a dumb old—" Then his eyes widened. "Oh, crap. He wouldn't, would he?"

"I don't know," I said. "You know what that shotgun looks like. Go see if it's in the bedroom. Alex, you look for Pepper."

I ran for the basement, praying I'd guessed wrong. But I hadn't. The cabinet door stood against the wall, its hinges neatly unscrewed, while boxes and boxes of shotgun and rifle shells lay strewn across the laundry table. For a second I froze, then I started scooping up loose shells and jamming them in boxes, as if getting everything back in the cabinet could change things. Behind me I heard Mom's hurried footsteps on the stairs. She stopped and stared, then sat down heavily on the steps. "Ducks," she said. "I should have known."

I let loose shells dribble slowly and pointlessly from my fingers into a box, then stood leaning against the table. Under my bathrobe, I could feel my armpits slippery with sweat. "Mom, what are we going to do?"

Her voice was tired. "I don't know. Maybe Bob will have an idea."

Bob Marston, the guy with all the answers. Or at least some answers, now that Dad no longer bothered with questions, answers, or any of that stuff.

Bob showed up a few minutes later in his fancy car. (Hey, look at me; I'm so successful I'll bet you just want to puke.) Mom went outside to talk to him, while I watched through the window and the boys shuffled around. Bob lifted his hands and let them drop, and Mom bowed her head like she was about to cry. He put a hand on her shoulder, and she covered it with one of her own. I turned away and glared at the boys. "Why don't you find something to do?"

Alex shrugged. "Such as?"

There wasn't anything to do. Not about Dad, anyway. Bob told Mom that Dad could be hunting in any of a hundred places in the surrounding twenty or thirty miles. All we could do was wait and pray that he'd be all right.

Alex and I got some decent clothes on and walked down to the Lutheran church where we're supposedly members, even though we don't go very often. I guess I thought it might help, but I couldn't keep my mind on the service. Alex enjoyed it, especially the hymns since he likes to sing loud, even if he can't sing well. By the time we were walking home, he was as sunny as ever.

"What's with you?" I growled. "Don't you ever worry?"

He gave me a hurt look. "Sure, I worry."

"Then why don't you ever show it?"

He shrugged. "What do you want me to do? Go around looking worried all the time? I figure you and Sid got that covered."

"I don't look worried all the time!"

"Yes, you do."

"No, I don't!"

We were about to get really childish, but Alex shrugged again. "Suit yourself."

"I will," I snapped.

Jim Baxter, who used to work with Dad at the warehouse, was behind the wheel of our car when it turned into our driveway in the late afternoon. Dad got out of the passenger seat and reached into the back to pull out some dead birds. Phil Simonson, another of the warehouse guys, pulled in behind them in a small pickup. Pepper rode in the back, his front paws on the side and a big grin on his face. He looked very proud of himself.

Mom started for the kitchen door, then stopped herself and waited. Phil knocked and stepped inside. "Hi, Leslie. Uh, Ken and Jim are going to clean ducks. I said that sounded too much like work to me and that I was going to cadge a cup of coffee."

"Sure, Phil." She went to the pot. "Where did you run into Ken?"

"Well, I kinda wanted to talk to you about that."

"Do you take cream or sugar?" Mom asked.

"No, black's fine." He accepted a cup, took a swallow, and glanced at us kids.

"It's o.k.," Mom said. "The kids live with this as much as I do."

Phil nodded. "Well, Jim and I were hunting out of our blind on Blue Heron. We weren't doing so hot, but somebody in an old blind down the shore was doing real good. Bang, bang, bang, about five ducks one right after another. Trouble is, we only see one gun barrel poking out. Jim says, 'What the hell's going on here? If there's only one guy in there, he's way over the limit. I'm gonna go down and check.'

"But I'd seen your dog retrieving so I said, 'I'm pretty sure that's Ken Zarada's lab. And, hell, Ken's too much of a sportsman to shoot more than his limit. I'll bet he's got one of his boys along and they're trading off with the gun.' And Jim says, 'Well, that kid's one hell of a shot then. Let's check it out anyway.'" Phil looked down. "So we did, Leslie, and we found Ken sitting by himself with nine ducks spread out at his feet. That's three times the limit."

Mom sighed. "What did he say, Phil?"

Phil looked at her, his face pained. "He didn't say anything. He just sat there like a statue, not saying or seeing anything. Then, suddenly he comes to. He stares at us and says, 'What the hell are you doing here? This is my blind.' And he looks pretty threatening for a minute. But you know the way Jim's got with people. He just grins and says, 'Sure, Ken. And it's a good one too.'" Phil took another swallow of coffee. "Anyway, we try to make some conversation—just like in the old days, you know—then Jim says that we're quitting for the day and would Ken like some help carrying out his birds? I mean, cripes, we had to get him out of there before the warden showed up. Ken guessed that'd be all right, and we walked out to the cars. Jim asked if he could drive your Chevy, since he was thinking of buying a used one like it. I mean, Ken just didn't seem quite right to us, Leslie, and we weren't sure he should drive."

"You did the right thing," Mom said.

He nodded. "Anyway, Ken said he didn't care who drove. So we headed over here. That's about it, I guess."

"Thanks, Phil. We're grateful." He looked relieved. She picked up the coffee pot. "Would you like another cup?"

"No, this was enough to warm me up." He glanced into the garage. "Well, I guess we'll get home then. Thanks for the coffee." He hesitated with his hand on the doorknob. "Leslie, he can't shoot ducks like that again. I mean, we took a chance and covered up for him this time, but next time he might get nailed. And the fine for every duck over the limit is something like a hundred bucks."

"He shouldn't be hunting anymore, Phil. I would have stopped him if I'd known that he was even thinking about it. Thank Jim for me. You guys did just right."

"Ya, well, glad we could help. We'll see you."

Dad didn't have much to say when he came in. He ate a big supper, then fell asleep in front of the TV, Pepper snoring peacefully at his feet. Mom came into the kitchen while I was cleaning up the last of the dishes. "Tomorrow I'm going to call for an appointment at the clinic. It may be time for us to consider those tranquilizers."

"For us or for him?" I said, then looked down into the dishwater, my lower lip quivering.

She gave my shoulder a squeeze. "Keep your sense of humor, Shar. It helps." She took dishes out of the rinse water and put them in the drying rack. "So what do you think? You didn't like the idea of tranquilizers back in the spring."

"I never liked the idea of this whole darn thing."

She sighed. "I know. But we've got to do what's best for him. I think he's feeling pretty good physically, and that may be half the problem. He wants to do the things he used to love. I hate to see him lose the desire, but we can't have him getting in trouble."

"What will the tranquilizers do?"

"Slow him down some. Make him more placid."

"And drive him farther from us," I said, and felt the

old familiar lump in my throat.

She gave me a long look. "Maybe so. . . . Well, I'm going to talk to Bob about it."

I wanted to scream: Leave Bob out of this! He doesn't care about Dad. He doesn't care about this family. He's just after you! My God, can't you see that?

She wiped the last couple of plates and put them in the cupboard. She sighed. "Well, somebody's got to clean up the mess your dad made cleaning those ducks. I'll send the boys out. It's about time they started helping more around here."

I went to the garage to see what kind of cleaning supplies they would need and almost threw up when I saw the workbench covered with feathers, blood, and duck guts. He'd skinned the birds, cut out their breasts, and left their mangled corpses in a greasy mound next to a pile of severed heads and feet.

The boys came out the door grumbling. The sight of the workbench stopped them dead in their tracks. They looked around wide-eyed. "Oh, my God," Alex said. "I think I'm going to puke."

"Oh, it's not that bad," I said, my Mom imitation sounding shaky. "I'll get some cleaning stuff and we'll do it together. Why don't you find a garbage bag for those birds?"

I ran a dishpan of hot water and Lysol, kicking myself for saying that I'd help. I handed the pan and a stiff brush to Alex, then dug around under the sink for some rags. But instead of going outside right away, I stood by the phone for a long minute, then picked it up very carefully, covering the mouthpiece with my hand.

Bob was talking. "Well, the tranquilizers may help, but they're not going to produce any miracles. It's still going to be tough."

"I know," Mom said.

Bob took a deep breath. "Leslie, I've been wanting to say this for a long time; sooner or later you're going to have to think about some other options."

"I know what you're going to say, Bob, but I just can't think—"

"A lot of institutions are decent places these days. He's a veteran and the VA home at King is very nice. My uncle spent years there, and he loved it. It's not like you'd be throwing Ken in a dungeon."

"Oh, Bob, the money—"

"Maybe it wouldn't be so bad. SuperComp's insurance plan is one of the best in the country. I'm sure they'll pay at least some of the cost. And if you worked full-time you could make three times what you do now. You know that."

"Bob, I just can't deal with this right now." Mom was on the brink of tears. Why didn't she just hang up on the dumb jerk?

"Leslie, you've got to think about it. For the kids' sake and for yours." He took another deep breath. "Look, my boys and I went through a bad time after Janet died. But we made up our minds that her death wasn't going to ruin our lives. And you can't let Ken's problem ruin yours." He paused. "At least let me check into what arrangements could be made."

There was a long silence. I stood frozen, stunned by what he'd said and terrified that they'd catch me listening. Finally, Mom said, "We're going to try the tranquilizers first."

"Fine. I agree. But just let me check."

She hesitated. "All right."

I couldn't listen any longer. I set the phone in the cradle as gently as I could with my shaking fingers. Alex opened the door, his face white. "Shar, did you look in the backseat?"

On the far side of the garage, Sid was scrubbing the workbench so hard that it shook. Alex opened the back door of the car. The seat cover was streaked with mud, duck blood, and sticky feathers. "Enough to make you puke, isn't it?" he said.

"Just stop talking about puking, o.k?" I stepped back. "I think there's a bottle of cleaner for seat covers above the workbench. See if you can find it." I stood looking at the mess. A long feather—green, white, and black—stuck to a spot of blood. I pulled it free and ran a finger along the rippling edge. Poor duck. If you'd flown a little higher or a little faster, you could have made it. Made it all the way south where it never snows and the sun shines all winter long.

Later, Sid and I went to the basement and put all the shells back in the cabinet. I held the door while Sid started screwing the hinges back in place. He stopped. "This is dumb. What are we going to do next? Hide all the screwdrivers so he doesn't take the door off again?"

"Maybe we could use nails or something."

He gave me a disgusted look. "Come on. If he wants to get the damn shells, he'll figure out a way."

I nodded and set the door back on the table. We gazed at the long rows of ammunition boxes. "Get a big box," I said. "We'll find some other place to hide them."

I lay in bed a long time thinking about what Bob had said about putting Dad in an institution. Even the idea made me furious. Dad would never get better surrounded by sick and crazy people. I wouldn't let them do it to him—not even after this weekend. Maybe all Dad needed were a few tranquilizers to ease him over the rough spots on the way to getting really well. I tried to believe that, tried to pray for a miracle, but somehow God seemed very far away and not much interested in our troubles.

Only when I was trying to fall asleep thinking of Paul did it occur to me that he hadn't called that evening.

He wasn't waiting by my locker when I got to school. My heart sprung a half dozen leaks and started sinking fast. But he caught me between first and second hours. "Hey, I'm sorry I didn't call last night. I got involved in the Brewers game on TV and kind of forgot."

"That's o.k. Did they win?"

"No, they lost in twelve. With four games to go, they're out of it."

"Too bad."

"Ya, with a little more pitching they could have won the division. Anyway, the stupid game took until midnight, and I didn't get up until ten to eight. That's why I missed you this morning."

"Oh. . . . Are you going to walk me home?"

I thought he hesitated just a split second. "Sure. I'll see you in biology."

In algebra, I chewed on a thumbnail as Mr. Barlow handed back our unit tests. Had I just imagined Paul's hesitation? I flipped over my test paper, and my breath caught. C minus? There had to be some mistake. Heck, I always got B's in math. I checked the scoring. No mistake. He was right and I'd been wrong—a lot. Just careless stuff. Darn. I'd better start concentrating more.

But I didn't. Instead, I spent the next couple of

classes with my mind only a tenth on what was going on, while the other ninety percent worried. I had to talk to Paul, had to explain things better, without crying and making a fool of myself this time.

I sat a little apart from my usual crowd at lunch, trying to get in the right frame of mind to act cheerful when I saw Paul in biology. "Hey, Shar, did you hear?"

I looked at Pam Corvitz. "Hear what?"

"Today's the big day, our first dissection."

"Oh, God," I said. "What are we going to cut up?"

"Big long worms of some kind. Everybody says they're real slimy and just full of formaldehyde."

"You can do the cutting. I'll take notes."

"No way. We made a deal; we split everything even."

"I didn't mean it."

"I did. Come on; it's nearly time for the bell."

Paul grinned and waved from his table on the other side of the room where he and Glen Foote were laying out their instruments. If only I'd agreed to be Paul's partner when he'd first asked. Pam picked up our tray and lab report form from Mr. Munrow and brought them over to the table. We stared at the worm. "Ugh," she said.

"Well, let's get it over with." I reached into the tray for the worm. "O.k. What's the first step?"

Paul met me outside the main door after the last bell. "How'd the dissection go?" he asked.

"O.k. Better than cleaning up a lot of disemboweled ducks."

"Huh?"

"I'll tell you later. Let's get away from all the people."

Actually, I hadn't minded the dissecting nearly as much as I'd feared. Pam had such a fit about touching the worm that I'd ended up doing most of the work. Now I felt tough—tough enough to quit being squeamish about a lot of things. I'd give Paul the rundown on Dad in a cool, businesslike fashion, then we'd get back to having some fun.

Yep, that's what I said to myself, and immediately turned into a blubbering idiot. We sat in the park near school while I tried to explain things to him, but I just couldn't. Not so they made any sense. He sat with his arm across the back of the bench, not saying anything while I cried.

When I finally got control of myself, I said, "Paul, just stick with me for a little while, huh? Everything's going to be o.k."

"Sure," he said.

Mom held up a bottle of orange pills. "These are what the doctor gave us. Your dad's supposed to take them three times a day. I'll give him one at breakfast, you give him one when you get home from school, and I'll give him the last one at bedtime."

"Will he object?"

"We'll have to see, but I kind of doubt it."

"Why?"

"I just do. That's all the reason I've got. Now I also talked to one of the psychiatrists today, and tomorrow she's going to try to explain to him why it's dangerous for him to drive or go hunting. I'm going to write you an excuse so you can come home at noon while we're at the clinic. I want you to get all that ammunition out of the basement and—"

"It's not in the basement, it's under my bed. Sid and I moved it there last night."

She looked at me in surprise. "Oh? Well, I don't care

for that much. Anyway, get it all in a box and give it to Bob when he comes about twelve-thirty."

"I don't think Bob knows anything about guns and bullets and stuff. Why not Phil or one of the other guys from the warehouse?"

"It doesn't matter whether Bob knows about guns and bullets or not. All he's going to do is store the box in his basement."

"The klutz will probably drop it and blow himself up. I think you should call Phil."

The blue of her eyes turned a colder shade. "Shar, I don't know what's behind this dislike you're building for Bob Marston. But knock it off. He's a good man and a good friend."

I stared at the tabletop. "How about the guns? Should I give him those too?"

"One thing at a time. Unloaded guns aren't going to hurt anybody."

"But, Mom, Dad can go downtown any old time and buy more shells."

"I know, but we can't push this thing too fast. We'll try to get rid of the guns soon. But not tomorrow."

I had the box sitting by the back door when Bob came up the walk from his car. "Hi," he said. "Beautiful day, huh?"

I glanced at the blue autumn sky. "I guess."

"This all of them?" He hefted the box. "Gosh, there must be enough here to start a war."

I shrugged. "I guess if you shot some of the right people. I'd start with real estate agents."

His smile wavered. "Oh? Why?"

"Just to slim down the competition for Mom, I guess."

His smile came back full force. "She does o.k. Better than o.k. You should be—"

"Ya, I know. Proud of her. We are. Excuse me, I've got to get back to school."

"Want me to drop you off? It's on my way."

"No, thanks. I'd rather walk." I wouldn't be seen in the same car with you if it was forty below, you jerk. "O.k. See you later." He lugged the box to his car. I half hoped he really would drop it and blow himself into a trillion pieces.

That afternoon I gave Dad his tranquilizer with a glass of Kool-Aid. He took it without complaint. Nor did he seem to mind when I gave him his pill the next day and the day after. It was a little hard to see what effect they had on him at first, but by Thursday he'd started to look sleepy a lot of the time. When I passed near him, he didn't look up but just kept on gazing at the TV picture and humming his soft tuneless hum.

Cindy called that night. "Sharzar, if you don't mind, I'm going to get a ride to school tomorrow."

"Why? Aren't you feeling good?"

"Oh, I'm feeling great." She giggled. "There's this guy who wants to give me a ride. I didn't tell you this, but Mark and I have kind of broken up over him."

"Oh? Who's the guy?"

"A friend of Mark's. Well, maybe ex-friend now. Do you remember when Mark and I went with that other couple to the dance in Hartlin?"

"Sure, I remember."

"Well, I really liked the guy who drove and he liked me. We danced together a lot until his girl got kind of mad. His name is Burt Kaiser. Burton, isn't that romantic? Well, he dropped by a couple of nights ago and asked me to go for a ride. He's broken up with his girl and thinks we ought to see what we've got in common. And I agree."

"How's Mark taking that?"

"Oh, he's pretty mad, but he'll get over it. I told you that he was just a stand-in until I found that guy with the red Camaro."

"Burt's got a red Camaro?"

"No, dummy. But he's got a blue Pontiac. That's a step in the right direction."

I hesitated. "How old is this guy, Cindy?"

"He's a junior. Just a couple of years difference."

"Well, you watch yourself, o.k.?"

"Sure thing. And you watch out for Mark. He's going to be on the prowl."

"Not for the likes of me."

"Confidence, girl. We're moving up in the world."

Maybe she was, but I wasn't sure what direction I was going in. I clumped through the rest of the week, paying only enough attention to get by in school, and letting my diet slip at home. Next week, I told myself, I'll get back on track. Paul took me to the football game at the high school Friday night, but it was colder than the week before and not nearly as much fun. I saw Cindy and a tall dark-haired guy at a distance. She looked very happy.

It started drizzling late in the game, and we left early to catch the bus home. It was pouring when we got off at the stop nearest my house, and we had to run the last two blocks. We were out of breath by the time we made it to the back porch. I shook water from my curls and tried to laugh. "Brrrr. Well, you said you liked curly hair. Now it's really going to be curly."

He wiped water from his face. "Ya, I guess so."

"Do you want to come in for a while? We could make some cocoa."

"Uh, I don't know, Shar. I'm cold and I don't want to drip all over your mom's floor. I think I'll just go home."

I hesitated. "So, am I going to see you tomorrow?"

He shifted uncomfortably. "I've kind of got some other plans. I'm sorry, I should have told you before. It's, uh, something with the family."

"Oh."

"I'm sorry. Maybe we can do something Sunday afternoon."

"I'd like that."

We stood awkwardly for another moment, all our ease with each other gone. He bent to kiss me. "I'll see you, huh?"

I put a hand behind his head and pulled him down to give him one that would really make him miss me. But he pulled away before I could get the job done. He laughed sheepishly. "I'm sorry. I just get worried about your da— Uh, about one of your parents catching us. Gosh, I'm cold. I'll call you."

And then he was gone, hurrying down the rainy street in the dark.

Saturday afternoon, Mom took Dad along when she went to look at a new housing development on the other side of town. Alex and Sid were at the park playing football, and I was left without much to do. I decided to bake some cookies. Heck, as long as I rationed myself, a few cookies wouldn't do any harm. Maybe I'd take a few to Paul's. Just put them on the doorstep with a note, ring the bell, and run. He'd have to call to say thanks.

I was mixing dough, Pepper at my side hoping for a handout or an accident, when the back door slammed open. Sid stomped in, followed by Alex. Sid grabbed a paper towel from the roll beside me and held it to his bleeding nose.

"Sid, what happened? Are you hurt bad?"

"It's just a bloody nose. Don't have a fit, huh?"

I reached for the paper towel. "Let me see."

"No." He swung away.

"How'd it happen?"

"We were playing football. It just happened, that's all." He threw the blood-sopped towel in the waste-basket, grabbed another, and stalked out.

I could tell by the look on Alex's face that Sid hadn't told the truth. "What really happened?" I asked.

He shrugged. "We were playing football like he said. Five guys on a team and having a good time. But you know how Sid gets wild sometimes, especially when something's eating on him. He started getting a little lippy and blocking a little too hard and covering passes a little too tight. And there's this guy on the other team who's got a short fuse and new blue jeans. Sid goes out to cover him on a pass and ends up knocking him down in a big mud puddle. It was no big deal, except for the kid's new jeans. Anyway, he jumps up and gives Sid a push. And even though the guy's a lot bigger, Sid ain't about to back down. So, they duke it out." He grimaced. "It just took a second for the kid to deck Sid. Pow, right in the nose. That was the end of it."

"Do you think his nose is broken?"

"Naa. He let me wiggle it. It's o.k., but it's going to look like a banana tomorrow."

108

I hesitated, then got a tray of ice out of the freezer, emptied it into a towel, and took it to the twins' room. I knocked on the door. "Sid, I brought you some ice." There was a moment's silence and then he came to the door. He kept his eyes down, and for the second time I could remember, I knew he'd been crying. I handed him the towel. "Thanks," he said. "Did Alex tell you what really happened?" I nodded. "Are you going to tell Mom?"

I hesitated. I probably should. "No. I'll just tell her that you caught an elbow by accident."

"Thanks."

"Sid," I said, "don't fight anymore, huh? If everything's really getting to you . . . Oh, heck, I don't know. Just run around the block or something. But don't fight."

He looked at me. "Ya, and what do you do?"

I felt tears come to my eyes, but I felt like laughing at the same time. "It's easier being a girl. I just cry."

He smiled almost shyly. "Ya. Maybe that's easier. At least you don't get your nose almost busted." He made an awkward gesture with the towel full of ice. "Thanks, Shar. This will help."

I'm not sure Mom really believed Sid or me, and we had an edgy supper. I wanted to get out of the house, but I didn't have a date and I hadn't thought to call any girl friends. I looked at Sid and Alex. "Do you guys want to go to a movie?"

They both looked at me in surprise—I probably hadn't taken them to a movie since *Bambi*. Alex said, "What happened to whatshisname?"

"Whatshisname is busy," I said. "Do you want to go or not?"

Alex shrugged. "Sure. What do you say, Sid?"

"Beats staying home."

We walked downtown. I wasn't real thrilled about being seen with my kid brothers on a Saturday night, but at least we'd gotten Alex out of the house before Mom made him tell her the real story of Sid's bruised nose. At the theater, the boys lied about their age so that we could get into a PG-13. We bought Cokes and the biggest vat of popcorn, then found some good seats. I put my knees up on the seat in front of me and waited for the lights to go down.

Paul walked in with Lori Durrell. The shock of pain that went through me was like nothing I'd ever imagined. I gaped, then slid down in my chair and hid as well as I could behind my jumbo container of Coke. Alex said, "Hey, isn't that—"

Sid snapped, "Stuff it, you jerk."

Alex looked at me. "Shar, wasn't that—"

"I didn't see him. Shut up and pass the popcorn."

The lights went down a few seconds later. I sat in the dark, the movie just color and motion before my eyes, and felt big tears slide down my fat cheeks.

Fifteen minutes before the movie ended, I whispered to Sid, "I'll meet you guys down the street." He nodded.

The night was sharp with the smell of frost and dead leaves. I sat in the little park with the statue of the long-dead soldier looming above me in the dark. Sid and Alex came down the block. Alex was laughing and making motions with his hands. Sid walked head down, hands in his pockets.

"Shar, you really missed it," Alex called. "That was the coolest ending. Indiana Jones . . ." He described the movie's finish as we walked. Finally, the task got too much for him. "Anyway, it was just too cool." He smiled and shook his head at the memory, bouncing along until he was a few steps ahead of us.

Sid put an arm awkwardly around me for a moment. "Hang in there, sis. We'll make it yet."

"I want to find that kid who slugged you. I feel like beating the crap out of somebody."

Sid didn't laugh. "I know what you mean, but I don't know where he lives." He gazed after Alex. "Well, there's always Alex. Let's just pound him so we can all feel like shit."

And we broke out laughing, sounding a little too crazy. Alex turned. "Hey, what's the joke, guys?"

"You wouldn't understand," Sid said.

Chapter 7

I walked down to the lake through wet grass and morning mist. A flock of ducks rose flapping and quacking off the water, circled once to pick up stragglers, then disappeared over the trees on the far side of the lake.

I laid my denim jacket on the grass and sat waiting for the sun to rise over the treetops. I was sick of crying, sick of worrying half the night, and sick of not noticing things that used to make me happy. Fall was slipping by. Tomorrow the sun wouldn't shine quite so warm and the colors in the trees would lose a little of their glow. I needed to store up the warmth and the color against the times ahead, when there would be only bare branches, cold, and snow.

A twig lay near my feet. I picked it up and started breaking off small pieces. O.k., I'd been dumped on by a boy. A boy who'd made me very happy for a few weeks. So what was I supposed to expect? Eternal love and endless patience from my first boyfriend? Besides, I'd known it was coming, known it ever since Dad had smashed his plate on the ground and started yelling. Paul wasn't to blame. I was. I'd driven him away with all my tears, complaints, and fumbled explanations.

The twig snapped in my fingers. But he'd lied to me! Said his family had plans when he was planning on taking out Lori Durrell. God, that burned me. Both the lying and Lori. Maybe she was slender and—what was that word Cindy used? Chippy. O.k., Lori was slender and chippy. But she was also dumb and didn't have the greatest reputation in the world. Oh, nothing real terrible, but I figured that she'd had her first cigarette, beer, joint, and roll in the clover a long time ago. And quite a few since. What the heck would Paul want with her?

What they all want, Sweetie, a voice inside me said—a voice that sounded suspiciously like Cindy's. No, not Paul; he wasn't like that. Oh, yes he is, the voice teased. Well, all right then; if he wanted some slut, let him have her.

I didn't mean that. I wanted Paul, wanted him more than I ever had before. I put both hands deep in my curls and rubbed my scalp furiously. Get the dumb thoughts out, Shar. O.k., look. He went out with Lori, but maybe they had a lousy time. Maybe he'll call this afternoon. He might even tell you about his date and apologize. And you can be real cool and say: "Oh, yes. I saw you at the movies. We were sitting a few rows behind you guys." Ya, that'd get him. He'd fumble: "Oh, you were there, huh? Uh, who with?" And maybe I'd tell him the truth or maybe I'd just say, "Oh, nobody you really know." Ya, I'd make him sweat a little before taking him back.

Suddenly, my eyes stung with tears. It'd never happen. Not a chance. Lori was fun, I wasn't. Lori was slender, I wasn't. And Lori would let him move a lot faster than I would. Oh, crap. I wanted my boy back, and I couldn't think how I'd ever get him.

I got up, swung my jacket over my shoulder, and started walking. The quivering-Jell-O part of me wanted to break down, wanted to call Paul on the phone and whimper and beg for him to give me another chance. But another part of me, the part that had gotten me through the last six months, snarled: Where's your pride, girl? He calls you, you make him squirm. And if you take him back, you set some conditions. And the first is no Lori or you'll break both his legs.

A lone duck flapped overhead, dipping to glide over the lake. For a second she seemed to hesitate, trying to decide whether to land or not. Then her wings began beating again and, with a couple of mournful quacks, she vanished into the morning blue beyond the trees.

I never quite decided what to do. In the end, it didn't make a lot of difference: Paul didn't call me. And I didn't call him. Instead, I sat with Dad watching the baseball playoffs, not caring if anyone ever won.

I was surprised when Cindy arrived at the door on Monday morning. She was wearing blue jeans, a blue turtleneck, and an angry expression. "Hi," I said. "No ride from Burt today?"

"No. Come on, you've got to do something for me on the way to school."

Out of sight of our house, she lit a cigarette. "When'd you start that?" I asked.

"This summer at camp. I quit when I got back, but I started again this weekend."

"Dumb habit."

"Aren't they all," she said. She shoved a note at me. "Here. I need you to sign this with my mom's signature."

"What is it?"

"An excuse to get out of gym. I forgot to get her to sign it."

"What's the matter?"

"Cramps. My period's about to start."

"Oh." I steadied the note on the back of my purse and took a pen from her. Then I paused. "Wait a second, you're way early. Or way late. We always have our periods about the same time. Let's see, mine was over . . ."

"Will you just sign the damn note?"

I stared at her. She glared back. "No. Because I think you're lying to me."

She tightened her lips, then reached up and pulled down the top of her turtleneck to show a big purple hickey on her neck. "There. That's the real reason. Damn Burt got carried away, and I don't want anybody in gym to see this. It's been hell enough keeping it from my parents."

"Wow," I said. "That is some hickey."

"Sharzar, will you please just sign the note?"

"O.k." I signed my nearly perfect imitation of her mom's signature. "Well, I haven't lost the touch."

She stuffed the note in her purse. "Thanks."

I know her problem shouldn't have made me feel better, but it did a little. I mean, that was a hickey and a half. "Cindy, I've always been a little curious. How do people get those? I mean, does—"

She almost started crying. "Just give me a break, Sharzar. Some other time, huh?"

"Oh, ya. Sure."

Paul had shoved a note through the lower vent on my locker. "Shar, Sorry I didn't call yesterday, but something came up. See you in biology. Paul."

I thought about it all morning and during lunch hour locked myself in a stall in the john to write a reply: "If by something, you meant someone, you can stop lying. I saw you and Lori at the movies Saturday night. Hope you had a good time. I hear she knows some killer knock-knock jokes. Shar. P.S. If you want to walk me home, fine. If not, that's also fine. Don't expect me to wait." I folded the paper, wrote his name on the outside, and made sure I got to biology first. I left it on his lab table and went to my own. He came in a couple of minutes later, and I watched out of the corner of my eye as he opened it. His face turned a satisfying shade of crimson.

Pam brought our tray to the table. "What's on the menu?" I said.

"Some kind of crab," she said. "I think this is the beast that put Meg's brother off tuna fish for life."

"Hand me that sucker," I said. "I feel like cutting on something."

"Be my guest," she said.

Paul didn't meet me in our usual place after school. I gave him ten seconds to show up and then started down the street. Passing the parking lot, I spotted Cindy standing next to a blue Pontiac talking to the tall dark-haired guy behind the wheel. She started away, and he reached out for her arm. She hesitated and turned back. Watch out, Cindy, I thought. But it wasn't my business, and I kept going.

I missed Paul a lot over the next few days, but I tried not to let it show either in school or at home. I knew one of the twins must have told Mom, but she didn't ask me any questions. Once when I caught her watching me, I said, "It's o.k., Mom. It hurts like hell, but I'll live." She nodded.

Maybe half the girls in school were wearing men's ties under their V-necked sweaters before I noticed the fad.

Get with it, Shar. No time to be different. When I got home that day, Dad was asleep in front of the TV, his big bowl on his lap and Pepper stretched out at his feet. Pepper lifted his head, saw it was only me, and put his head back on his paws. I slipped into the den and dug through the ties in the back of the closet until I found a dark red one I liked. I tried it on in front of the mirror in my room, knotting it loosely then pulling a sweater over my head. It looked like crap. Maybe a brighter red would work. I went back to the den.

I was sorting through the ties again when I brushed against something heavy in the pocket of an old coat. What the hey? I stuck a hand in and felt a round cylinder. My blood froze. A shotgun shell. How long had it been there? And why? I shoved it in my jeans pocket, grabbed the nearest tie, and hurried out of the den. Dad and Pepper were still asleep.

That evening I asked Mom to come to my room. I sat on my bed and she sat on my chair. I think she was expecting me to tell her about Paul dumping me. Instead, I handed her the shotgun shell and told her where I'd found it. "Mom, what are you going to do?"

She gazed at the shell, then slowly folded it in her palm. "Give it to Bob, I guess."

"But maybe Dad's got some more hidden, Mom."

"Maybe. What do you want me to do about it?"

I stared at her in exasperation. How could she be so stupid? "Get rid of the guns, Mom! That way it won't make any difference if he's got shells or not."

"We will in time. Right now he won't hear of it. I know."

"But, Mom, it's not his right—" I broke off, not sure what I was trying to say.

Her cool blue eyes probed me. "Not his right to do what?"

"I don't know," I said miserably. "He just shouldn't have those guns around."

"He was brought up around guns, Shar. He's the most unlikely person in the world to have an accident with a gun. Even now."

"But how about the day he went hunting? You were frantic."

"Not quite."

"Well, you were real worried."

"Not about him having an accident with a gun."

"What were you so worried about, then? And don't tell me it was just because he was driving the car."

"No, it wasn't just that." She didn't say anything for a long minute. "Shar, underneath everything your dad isn't very happy. He knows he's lost something and he's tried to find it again. But he can't. All those good feelings are gone forever." She paused, and I knew she was watching me but I wouldn't meet her eyes. "Now let's just suppose that he gets so unhappy that he doesn't want to go on living. What do you think he might do?" I shook my head, refusing to answer. She went on, her voice as cool and controlled as ever. "I think, Shar, that he might decide to stop living. Do you think we'll be able to stop him? Or that we'll even have the right—"

"You just don't love him anymore!"

She sighed. "Yes, I do, Shar. I love him as well as I can. I care for him, I provide for him. And I'll keep doing it as long as I'm able. But, Shar, your dad—the Dad we all remember loving—isn't coming back. He's gone forever. We've got to accept that."

I glared at her, my eyes burning with tears. "How can you be so cool about everything?"

Her voice hardened. "Because I've got to be! Do you think I could make it through a single day if I gave in to all the pain I feel? Shar, I've got to be tough! I've got to be tough for you and the boys—and for him. And, you've got to get tough too, Shar. You can't let every little thing throw you into a tizzy." She held up the shotgun shell. "This is a shotgun shell. That's all. Now maybe he was saving it in case he wanted to go duck hunting again. Or maybe he put it in that pocket a couple of years ago and forgot about it. Or maybe he was hiding it because he might want to use it on himself someday. We don't know! Now I'm going to get rid of it. And when I can get those guns out of the house without creating a major upset, I'll do that too. But right now, we're just going to keep going day to day. Understand?"

I sat with my knees drawn up to my chin, not looking at her. She hesitated, then said softly, "That is all we can do, Shar." She leaned forward to give me a quick hug and a kiss on the curls. "Hang in there. Just try to keep the pain from taking over. Things will get better."

She was at the door when I said, "Mom, can't we keep him from getting so unhappy? So unhappy that he might—" I couldn't get the words out.

She put her hand on the doorjamb as if she suddenly needed support. "All we can do is do the best we can for him." She turned, all the surface cool gone from her eyes, leaving pain a mile deep. "And, Shar, when he does die—whatever the cause—we're going to bury him. But we're not going to be burying the man we loved. He's already dead, Shar. He died last spring when that artery broke in his brain. We've got to remember that. We simply have to."

Easy for her to say. She had confidence and looks and her job. She had Bob Marston panting after her, ready to come any time she whistled. She had me to keep the twins in line and do all the work around the house. Me, the dutiful daughter who'd gotten herself so screwed up that she couldn't even keep a boyfriend for a month. But for Mom life wasn't all that complicated. And if Dad blew his brains out, life would be just that much simpler for her.

I guess I didn't really believe that crap, but I sure felt like I did for a while.

I went to the mall with Cindy on Thursday—the first time we'd really done anything together in maybe a month. I tried on jeans again, sucking in my gut and trying to kid myself that my old size still fit. "God, I've got to lose some weight," I said.

She glanced at my bulging waist. "It wouldn't hurt." I gave her a wounded look, and she let out an exasperated sigh. "Oh, come on, Shar. You said, 'I've got to lose some weight' and I said 'It wouldn't hurt.' Don't make like I called you an elephant or something. The jeans look fine. Now buy them or don't buy them. But hurry up; I've got to go to the bathroom."

I bought them, swearing that I'd lose enough weight to make them fit right.

In the rest room, Cindy put on lipstick while I dug in my purse. "Darn, I must have forgotten my hairbrush at school. Can I use yours?"

"Sure." She gestured at her open purse.

I pawed through the bushel of stuff she always has in her purse. Two thin tinfoil packages caught my eye, and without thinking I pulled them out for a closer look. My stomach flipped over. "Cindy! Where'd you get these . . . these whatchacallems?" Condoms, dummy. God, they advertise them on TV now.

She glanced my way and her face went pale. "Put those back! You weren't— You weren't supposed to see them."

"But, Cindy, you and Burt aren't—"

"Don't be dumb. I'm just, uh, holding them for someone."

"Who?"

"Just someone."

I stared at her. She was trying to fake calm as she started touching up her eye shadow, but her fingers were shaking. "Cindy, tell me the truth."

She let her hands drop and stared at herself in the mirror for a long moment. "O.k.," she said. "They're mine. Burt and I haven't done it, but he wants to. I'm still thinking about it. But if I decide that I want to, I'm going to make him wear one."

"Cindy, I don't think you should even be thinking about doing it. You're only—"

"Oh, grow up, Shar! Lots of fourteen-year-old girls aren't virgins and haven't been for a long time. And just because you decide to do it with a guy doesn't make you some kind of slut. Not if you care about the guy. And it doesn't ruin you for life either. Now put those things back in my purse and stop looking at me that way." She turned back to the mirror, angrily brushing away a couple of tears that threatened to wreck her eye shadow.

I hesitated, then put the condoms into her purse and zipped it shut. "They're right on top. Maybe you'll want to find a better place to hide them."

"Thanks, I will."

"Cindy, I don't think I know you anymore," I said quietly.

She spun. "Well, I don't think I know you either! I haven't been able to talk to you since I got back from

121

camp. I try to have a little fun and all you do is mope around like there's this little black cloud always dumping rain on poor Shar. You're about as much fun to be around as . . . as some kind of constipated bear or something. God, no wonder you couldn't hold onto Paul. Maybe Lori isn't real bright, but at least—"

I didn't wait to hear the rest. I was out the door and half running down the hall toward the outside door.

Cindy was crying when she called that night. "Sharzar, I'm sorry. I didn't mean all that stuff. Especially about you and Paul and Lori. God, I was awful to you. Forgive me, huh?"

I blinked back tears of my own. "I know you didn't, Cindy. It's o.k."

"Are we still friends?"

"Sure. . . . But, Cindy, just be careful, huh? I mean with Burt."

"I will. That's why I've got those, uh, you know. Those things. And I'm not going to do it just because he wants me to. But I want to be prepared just in case. You can understand that, can't you, Sharzar?"

"Yes," I said. I took a breath. "It was just kind of a shock, you know. I didn't think that we were going to . . . Oh, heck. I just didn't know it was something that we had to start thinking about yet." There was a long pause. She was still crying. "I've got to go," I lied. "I'll talk to you tomorrow."

Alex came into the kitchen. "Done with the phone?" I nodded and went to the refrigerator while he punched out a number from memory.

"Hello, Paul? Alex, here. Hey, my brother and I are trying to put together another one of those toothpick

bridges. Could you tell me how to test it again. . . ?
Right. . . . Hey, that'd be great. In the science room before school tomorrow. We'll be there. . . . Shar? Oh,
she's fine. . . . Ya, I will." He hung up the phone and
started for the door. "Paul says hi," he said.

"Hi to him too," I said.

My own brothers chumming with my ex-boyfriend!
Finks.

We almost bowled each other over coming around the
corner next to the teachers' parking lot. "Oh, hi," Paul
said.

"Hi," I said.

"Uh, how you doing?"

"O.k. And you?"

"Fine," he said.

We stared at each other. And I asked what I'd sworn
I'd never ask. "Paul, will you just tell me why?"

He shuffled. He was good at that. "I don't know,
Shar. It just didn't seem to be working out."

"Is it working out better with Lori?" Will you shut up,
Shar!

He shrugged. "I don't know. She's fun, I guess."

Well, whoopee. "Good for her," I said and turned
away.

"Shar, I just got scared, that's all. I mean, I liked you a
lot. Like you a lot." I turned to look at him again. Please,
Paul. Oh, please. "But, you see, I'd kind of counted on
you to show me how to . . . I don't know. Have a
girlfriend, I guess. Then all the other stuff came up,
and I just didn't know how to handle it."

I bit my lip. "I know. It was my fault. I shouldn't have
laid all that on you. And, Paul, I'm sorry about that

dumb note. . . . I was just kind of mad that you lied to me."

He stared at his feet. "Ya, I felt lousy about that. But I didn't know how to handle that either."

I swallowed the last of my pride. "Paul, will you call me sometime? Just to talk."

"Sure, I could do that. But . . . Well, you see, Lori and I are—"

"Don't tell me about that. Just call sometime, o.k.?" I hurried off.

On the walk home, I ran that dumb little conversation through my head a dozen times. Had he seen how close I'd come to throwing myself on my knees? Or had I just shown that I was willing to patch things up? And did I really care what he thought as long as the door was still open a crack? Lori. God, how could I win him back from that fun, slender, chippy little slut? Well, I certainly wasn't going to do it by letting myself get sadder and fatter. I had to get back on my diet before I became this gloomy mountain of flesh oozing down the hallways, swallowing up anything and anybody in its way.

I got Dad's tranquilizer from the closet over the sink and took it to him. He was staring at the Smurfs on TV. "Dad, here's your pill." For a few seconds he didn't react, and I thought I might have hit him in the middle of a blackout. Then he turned slowly and seemed to take a long time focusing on me. He lifted his hand at the speed of a sloth reaching for a banana, took the pill, and just as slowly guided it to his mouth. The Smurfs went to a commercial and were back on again before he'd washed it down with Kool-Aid and settled himself again. The little blue creatures hopped about and sang their songs in their wonderful little world where a not-very-terrible magician and his even-less-frightening cat were the only threats to happiness. If only I could send Dad into that world where the Smurfs would keep him safe and happy always.

Chapter 8

I sat home Friday night. Alex asked if I wanted to go to the movies, but I wasn't about to risk running into Paul and Lori. Cindy didn't call Saturday morning to ask if I wanted to go shopping. I wasn't surprised. She'd apologized and I'd forgiven her, but I knew that things could never be the same between us.

Mom was up. Way up. She and Bob had been chosen to lead the sales campaign for the new and very ritzy housing development on the east side of town. "Next weekend, we're having three houses open to the public, and we'll have to work like crazy to get ready. Do you have any plans for the weekend, dear, or can I count on you to hold the fort here?"

"I don't have any plans, Mom."

"Good. This is a real big break for me, Shar. For us. With a bit of luck, we'll be able to pay our bills and get ahead a little."

"That's great, Mom."

Bob's car pulled up to the curb. "Here's Bob. We're off to the printer's first. He's going to run our flier first thing Monday morning, and we want to make sure there aren't any bugs in it." At the door she turned. "Oh, I forgot to give your dad that darn pill. Can you do that for me, dear?"

"Sure, Mom."

She blew me a kiss and hurried out to the car. I sat looking at the gray skies beyond the kitchen window. I didn't have any weekend plans, and in her book that was good.

I brought Dad his pill and made sure he concentrated long enough to take it. Then I sat on the front steps for a while, watching a chill wind tumble leaves from the trees and blow them in eddies along the street. When I was good and cold, I went to my room, closed the door, and took off all my clothes. I studied myself in the mirror for maybe ten minutes until I was sure that I had no illusions left, then sat down at my desk and started writing out my reasons for sticking to a diet. It was cool in my room and I had goose bumps all over, but I wanted to remember my spare tire drooping and my big butt flattened against the cold chair.

The first item on my list was Paul, of course. I knew that my chances of winning him back were between slim—great word choice, huh?—and zip, but I'd have no chance unless I got my act together on the diet and a lot of other things. Another boy, came second. Fitting into my clothes again, third. And so on.

I heard a knock on my door. "Hey, Shar?" Sid called.

I half turned, automatically covering myself as well as I could. "Don't come in! What is it?"

"Uh, we're going out for awhile. If that's o.k."

"Where?"

"Oh, just a friend's."

"Well, how about coming back by one-thirty, huh? I might want to go somewhere this afternoon."

"Suppose we call?"

"Ya, o.k."

I'd lost my concentration, and I was freezing to death. I gave up on my list for the time being and started getting dressed. I pulled on panties over what I had too much of and my bra over what I had too little of, no matter what Cindy said, then got out a blouse nice enough for going to the mall. I peeked through the curtains to see the twins moving carefully up the block, a cardboard box balanced between them. And I knew instantly what was in it and why Sid hadn't quite told me where they were going. They weren't going to see just *some* friend, they were going to see *my* friend. A guy who was real interested in toothpick bridges but not much interested in me anymore. You dirty rotten finks, I thought. I hope you drop that damn box.

The door behind me opened and I spun to see Dad. He stared at me, at my naked legs and my unbuttoned blouse. I was alone with him, and he was very big and very near. And the thought I had staring into his dull eyes shook me to my toes. Am I what you want, Dad? Would it make everything better if you could have me here on this bed? Then go ahead, Dad, because I'll do anything, even that, if it will make you well again.

"Geese," he said. "I heard geese." He pushed by me, threw the curtains open and stared out the window. I didn't move, but stood for a long moment so close to him that I could feel the heat of his body. Then I grabbed my jeans and shoes, and clutching them to my belly, ran from the room.

I got sick in the toilet, then cried while I washed my face and tried to brush the taste of vomit from my mouth. I cried because I was scared, and even more because I knew that I wouldn't have fought him if he'd pushed me down on the bed, instead of standing at my window looking for geese flying south against the gray sky.

I called Paul's number. "Paul, let me speak to Alex."

"Oh, ya. Sure."

Alex came on the line. "Alex, I want you guys home by one. I've got to get out of here."

"Why? Is something the matter?"

"I'm just sick and tired of baby-sitting Dad. Can you understand that, or are you guys too damned selfish?"

He hesitated. "Gosh, Shar, you kinda lost me. We—"

"Just be here, huh? Now put Paul back on."

I waited. In the background I could hear Alex say something about me being "pissed off something fierce." Paul came on the line. "Paul, are you going to the mall this afternoon?"

"Well, no. I hadn't planned on it, anyway."

"Good, because I don't want to see you there. You or Lori. Or you and Lori. Got that?"

"Well, she's not even in town today, Shar. She's—"

"I don't give a damn where she is. You can both go to hell." I hung up.

I made Dad lunch, then sat across the table watching him while he ate in slow motion. What I'd thought for that instant before I'd run from the bedroom gnawed at me, but I pushed it away. Girl, you have got to get a grip on yourself. That or go completely crazy.

The boys showed up right at one, and I beat it.

Halloween decorations were up all over the mall. I walked around aimlessly. I didn't feel like shopping, and I didn't want to meet anyone I knew or who knew me or Dad or anyone I'd ever known. I wandered into the arcade and blew a couple of bucks trying to play a video game. I'd never been any good at them and had never cared either. But it was dark in the arcade with only the green lights of the screens illuminating the players' faces and all the whizzes, zaps, and bangs covering the human sounds. Maybe some guy I didn't know would come by and be friendly. Offer to help me learn the game and then take me for a Coke. Or maybe a drive in his car, down the road and far, far away.

But no one gave me a glance, and when I couldn't afford another game, I walked out, turned left, and pushed through the doors into the gray afternoon. I walked alone for two hours before going home.

The twins stayed out of my way until after supper when Alex approached me carefully. "Uh, Shar. Did Mom mention that we're invited to a slumber party tonight?"

"No."

"Is it o.k. if we go?"

"Just get out of here. I'll hold down the fort. As usual."

"Uh, right. Well, we'll see you tomorrow."

"Not if I see you first." Witty, Shar. Real witty.

Dad watched a TV movie in the family room, and I watched for Mom from the kitchen window. A couple of times, the memory of the crazy thoughts I'd had that morning crept into my head, but I pushed them away. Get a grip, girl. Time to stand up for yourself. And time, damn it, for Mom to start getting home in decent season, instead of expecting her fourteen-year-old daughter to hold down the fort all the damn time.

It was nearly nine when Bob's car pulled into the

driveway. They sat together for maybe five minutes while my anger heated up about a degree a second. Then I saw their two shadows suddenly merge and stay together for a long time. And I went cold all over.

She came in the door, her face flushed and smiling. "Hello, dear. Did everything go o.k?" I glared at her, then turned and stomped out of the room.

She came to my room a few minutes later. "Shar, what's the matter? Did your dad do something?"

"No, you did!"

"Me? What did I do?"

"You know."

"No, I don't. Tell me what's got you so upset, dear."

"I was watching from the kitchen window and I saw what you and Bob were doing. If you're going to get it on with him, Mom, I'd think you'd at least have the decency not to do it in our driveway!"

I guess I'd expected her to go white with shock, then to run crying from the room, unable to meet her daughter's eyes. Instead, her face went pink. "Don't you spy on me, young lady! Bob gave me a friendly hug, that's all."

"I don't believe that!"

"I don't care what you believe. I'm telling you what happened. And even if I did—as you so politely put it— get it on with Bob, that would be none of your damn business."

"Like hell it wouldn't," I yelled. "You're my mother and my dad's your husband. And he is *not* dead. Or have you forgotten that too!"

She gave me a look that came very close to hatred. "Oh, I haven't forgotten. I haven't forgotten about either one of you." She turned on her heel and walked out. I stared after her for a moment, then grabbed the door and slammed it as hard as I could.

I was lying on my bed crying when she knocked on my door an hour later and came in without waiting to be asked. I turned my face to the wall. She sat on my chair. "Look, Shar, I'm not having an affair with Bob Marston. When Bob hugged me tonight, it was just a friendly gesture. We'd had a really good day and we were pretty happy. I'm sure it looked strange, but it was innocent."

"How do I know you're telling me the truth?"

"I suppose you just have to believe me."

I wanted very much to trust her again, but it was so hard. "Mom, I see how he looks at you. And I'm old enough to figure out what he's feeling. He's in love with you, Mom!"

She sighed. "I know he is. But he's a very decent man, Shar. He wouldn't make a move unless I let him know it was o.k." She put a hand on my back and began rubbing slow circles. "Shar, it may be hard for you to understand this, but there wouldn't be anything so terribly wrong if I did let him. Your dad doesn't care anymore. I can take off all my clothes in front of him, and he looks at me like I'm not even there. That's something else that's gone from his life—from our life together. In bed, I'm just a hot-water bottle for him. And I miss being more, Shar. Sometimes I miss it very much."

I tried to curl myself in a ball, but she pushed down on my back for a second, her hand surprisingly strong. "Now just listen. To someone your age, sex sounds like an adventure. Half scary, half exciting. But when you're older, you start thinking about it more as a chance to be warm and relaxed with somebody. A chance to love someone for a little while and get comfort from his body. I don't have that with your father anymore. He's just not interested. How do you suppose that makes me feel? Well, I'll tell you. It makes me feel like I'm not a woman anymore. He doesn't care if I've got breasts and sex organs. He doesn't care that I've borne his children. Shar, he doesn't love my body anymore. And he doesn't love anything else about me either."

"Mom—"

"Let me finish. Now I'm not going to start jumping into bed with Bob every chance I get. I'm not going to go off on long weekends and leave you guys alone. But I'm going to keep on being friendly with him, because I like being with him and because he still knows I'm a woman." Her hand paused on my shoulder, and she pushed me gently over until I had to look at her. "And, Shar, if someday Bob and I decide to go to bed together, not you or anybody else will have any right to criticize us." For a long moment she stared steadily into my eyes, then she leaned forward and kissed me on the forehead. "Now go wash your face, then get some sleep. I love my big girl. Even when she doesn't love me."

After she left, I put my head back in my damp pillow and lay without moving for a long time, wishing I was about six years old and too young to know anything about men and women and what they could feel.

The next afternoon, I dropped Dad's tranquilizer down the garbage disposal. I just couldn't stand losing him to the pills any longer. Better to have him getting mad at me every once in a while. Or calling me short and fat or touching my breasts and legs like I was a walking hunk of meat. I turned on the water and let the disposal grind the pill into orange dust and wash it someplace far away where maybe it would give a fish a thrill. Then I went to the family room to try to get Dad interested in a game of checkers.

The first couple of days, I was cautious, watching him closely to see how much difference it made when I didn't give him his pill in the afternoon. He was grouchier and his movements were a little quicker, but he didn't get really mad and he didn't wander off. I worked with him every day. God, how I worked. I nagged him, tried everything I could think of to get him interested in something besides the darn TV.

I don't think Mom or the twins noticed anything different about Dad or how hard I was working to bring him back. They were too wrapped up in making millions selling real estate or in building indestructible bridges out of toothpicks.

School days seemed longer than ever. I got a C minus on a history report and a lousy D on an algebra test, but I no longer cared much about my grades. I didn't see much of Cindy and nothing of Paul except when I passed him in the halls. In the evenings, I tried to stick to my diet, but snacks seemed to appear magically in my fingers. To heck with it. As soon as I got Dad better, I'd worry about grades, friends, boys, and calories.

The week wore down. Friday came, and the only date I had was trying to interest Dad in playing checkers or cards. He wasn't, but he would be. Those things and a lot more. So help me God.

Mom was anxious about the weather Saturday morning. The big house-showing was scheduled to last all day and well into the evening, when there would be a wine and cheese reception for extra special prospects. She left early, wearing her best business suit and carrying her cocktail dress wrapped in plastic.

The rain held off until afternoon, when it started coming down steady and cold. The twins moped around, apparently sick of messing with toothpicks and glue. "Why don't you guys try to get Dad interested in a board game?" I asked. "He used to love them."

"What's the point?" Sid said.

Alex stepped in before I could take Sid's head off. "Ya, why don't we try it, Sid? Heck, there isn't anything else to do." Sid shrugged.

They couldn't keep Dad interested in the game and ended up playing by themselves until they also lost interest. I warmed up a frozen pizza and we ate. Alex studied the TV guide. "Hey, there's a Police Academy movie on. Maybe that would cheer everybody up."

Sid glanced over at the ad. "We've seen that one. Is there anything else?"

"A James Bond movie is on at seven. How's that sound, guys?"

No one objected. "Help me do the dishes first," I said.

Alex gets into productions every now and then. He made two batches of popcorn, got us all sodas, and hustled everyone into the family room in time for the start of the movie. Dad sat in his big chair, his big silver bowl on his lap, while the rest of us took places on the couch. Pepper sprawled on the rug in front of us, waiting for his share of the popcorn to hit the floor one way or another.

It was a good movie, lots of flashy boats, fast cars, and sunny Caribbean scenery. The boys really got into it, and I found myself actually enjoying something for the first time in a couple of weeks. I glanced at Dad every once in a while, and he seemed to be liking it too. Then right in the middle of this incredible chase scene, the screen flipped to an old black-and-white movie, then to a sitcom, and finally to a college football game. Dad set down the remote control with a satisfied grunt and leaned back in his chair.

"Come on, Dad!" Sid yelped. "That was the best part of the whole movie."

In a second I saw it all coming. "Sid, don't—" I yelled, but I was too late.

Sid grabbed the remote control from the arm of Dad's chair and tried to change the channel back to the movie. Dad's arm shot out like a big snake striking. "My TV," he roared. Sid tried to whirl away, but Dad grabbed his arm and jerked him off the couch.

"Dad, stop it," I screamed.

"Just give it to him, Sid," Alex yelled.

But neither one of them heard us. Sid tried to wrestle free, both hands clutching the remote. Dad shook him like a rag doll, then ripped the remote away with his other hand. Sid clawed for it. "Give me that, you big—"

With a snarl, Dad threw him halfway across the room. Sid landed hard, his head grazing the end table by the couch and knocking the lamp to the floor. The bulb popped. I think he was going to get up and charge Dad, but I grabbed him. Alex was down beside us, trying to tell Sid to forget the stupid movie. That's when Dad started making the sounds. He towered above us in the half-darkness, his hands working and his eyes blazing with something terrible. And all the while, these awful, wordless growls came from somewhere deep inside him. Then he spun and plunged for the bedroom that had once been his den and where he still kept his bowling trophies, fishing rods—and guns.

136

For what seemed like forever, I couldn't move—even with the thousand alarm bells screaming in my head. From his hiding place under the dining-room table, Pepper let out a whine of fear, and for some reason, that sound seemed to cut through whatever held me frozen. I jerked Sid to his feet and started dragging him toward the kitchen, my other hand pushing Alex in front of us. "Come on," I sobbed. "You've got to get out of here. He's got guns in there!" I shoved them through the back door into the rain. "Go find Mom. Don't come back until I call."

Sid grabbed my arm. "No! You're not staying here."

"I've got to," I sobbed. But the boys pulled me away and down the driveway to the street.

We walked across town in the drenching rain. We could have gone to Cindy's or maybe Paul's, or stopped any of a dozen places to use a pay phone to call Mom. But we just kept walking through the dark, cold rain until we got to the new housing development.

The light from the windows of a big house shone on the line of expensive cars parked along the unpaved street, and we could hear the laughter inside as we climbed the steps to ring the bell. Mom answered the door, looking very beautiful in her black cocktail dress. Her bright smile vanished. "My God," she said. "What happened?"

"Dad," I said. "We couldn't stay."

For an instant all the strength seemed to leave her and she swayed on her feet. But she took a deep breath and it all flooded back. "Come in out of the rain," she said. "You're soaked." The room went dead quiet when people saw us. "Go on with the party," Mom called. "It's nothing to worry about." She herded us into the kitchen. A couple of people from the catering service stared at us. "Has anybody seen Bob Marston?" she asked.

"Here I am." Bob came in from the room on the other side, still chuckling a little at what someone had said. He froze in his tracks.

"It's o.k., Bob," Mom said. "There was some trouble at home, but I can handle it. Just keep things going for a while. Show those slides of the developer's plans. I'll be with you in a few minutes."

He didn't hesitate. "Right. I got it." He put his smile back on and headed for the crowd. The catering people followed with their trays.

I started telling Mom what had happened, but Sid broke in, trying to take all the blame. But I had to tell her the truth and, when Sid finished, I did. "Mom, I stopped giving Dad his afternoon tranquilizers about a week ago. I just couldn't stand seeing him like—" I started bawling.

"Oh, my God," she breathed. "You love him so much." She pulled me close, then reached out her other arm for the boys. Crying and shivering against her beautiful dress, we huddled in the circle of her arms.

"It was my fault, not Shar's," Sid whispered.

Alex was sobbing. "I shouldn't have suggested the dumb movie."

"Hush," Mom said. "Hush, all of you. It's no one's fault. Not any of it." She hugged us tight, then pushed us away gently. "Now, I'm going back to work. We'll be done here in an hour."

"But, Mom," I pleaded. "Suppose he—"

"No buts," she said. "In an hour we'll go see how he is. If he's all right, then we'll go on just like before. If

138

he's—" She took a deep breath. "If he's not, then an hour won't make any difference. Now, go use the bathroom upstairs. There are some towels there. Everybody's already seen that part of the house, so you'll have it to yourselves. I'll come get you as soon as this is over."

We rode home in Bob's car. When Mom got out, he reached for her hand. "Call me later, huh?" he said. She nodded.

Pepper met us at the door. He grinned at us, then scooted by to do his business in the backyard. Alex, Sid, and I stood in our damp clothes in the middle of the kitchen, while Mom went through the family room to the den. She came back a minute later. "Asleep," she said. "Nothing more."

Chapter 9

Somehow we slept. A note lay on the kitchen table when I came down Sunday morning. "Kids, Bob and I took your father to the hospital. He didn't seem to mind. Home soon. Love, Mom."

They kept Dad in the psychiatric wing for a week, testing different medications. We visited him a couple of times, and he seemed o.k. We also had two sessions with a family counselor at the clinic. He got us talking about a lot of fears and hurts that we'd been hiding ever since the spring. It got pretty emotional, but I think we all felt a lot stronger afterward.

For the first time, we talked about putting Dad in an institution. Bob had done the checking, but the news wasn't so good. It would cost a lot, and Dad's health insurance from SuperComp wasn't going to help much. And, maybe none of us were quite ready to take the step anyway. I know Bob didn't agree with our decision, but he just grinned, as usual, and went on being helpful. Every time we needed him that week, he was there, and I began to understand how Mom felt about him.

I called Paul. "Paul, I'm sorry. I didn't mean that stuff I said on the phone. Don't go to hell on me." I bit my lip, hoping that came out a little like a joke.

"It's o.k. Alex told me things got a little rough on you guys for a few days."

"Ya, they did." I took a breath. "So, we're still friends?"

"Sure."

"Good. Because I really need to know that, Paul. Call me sometime, huh?"

"I will," he said.

That was all I could do about Paul and me. He'd call or he wouldn't, but either way, my heart was in one piece again. I went to my room and threw away my list of reasons for keeping to a diet—the list that had started with his name. Then I got out a clean sheet of paper and wrote in big letters: *For Myself*. There was no reason to add anything more; I'd learned that much, anyway. I taped it to the top of my mirror and gave myself a thumbs up. Low-cal, girl. All the way.

When Dad came home, he seemed better—calm but not so drugged out. He wasn't really Dad anymore, but he was about as good as we could hope. I'd cleaned the screen of the TV and vacuumed all the dirt, old popcorn, and stale chips out of his big chair. He sat down with a grunt of satisfaction, set his big silver bowl on his lap, and picked up the remote control. Pepper flopped down in his spot beside the chair and thumped his tail on the floor two or three times. I set a glass of Kool-Aid at Dad's elbow and went on about my life.

Halloween fell on the next Saturday, a fall day so warm and bright that you could almost forget any troubles at all. Mom had to work and the twins had plans, so I hung around the house most of the day, getting caught up on my homework and baking some cookies that I was going to let other people eat. But I didn't want to miss all the sunshine, so in the late afternoon I pulled on my denim jacket and headed for the back door. Then I hesitated. Well, it wouldn't hurt to ask. I went to the family room where Dad was watching another football game. "Dad, would you like to walk down to the lake? We might see some ducks."

He turned to look at me. I waited, used to that too by now. "I guess that would be o.k.," he said.

"I'll get your jacket."

We sat on the end of the dock, where so long ago Dad had taken the hook out of my thumb. I didn't chance asking if he remembered; I wanted to keep that memory just as it was. So we sat in the warm sun not talking, just being together as much as we ever could be again. Pepper nudged Dad's arm, and Dad lifted a big hand to scratch behind his ears. "He's a good dog," I said.

Dad nodded. "Ya, he's a good dog." He hesitated, then surprised me by going on. "No worries being a dog. Not as long as you get some food, a pat now and then, and maybe a chance to chase a rabbit once in a while. Not a bad life."

"I guess," I said. Dad looked over the lake, humming softly to himself. "Dad," I asked, "do you feel a little better now? I mean, since you came home from the hospital."

"I feel o.k. Better than that night when you kids left, I guess."

"You remember that, huh?"

"I remember."

"Dad, why'd you run to the den? What were you going to do?"

He didn't answer for a long minute, and I almost hoped he wouldn't. "I was going to get my shotgun."

"Why, Dad?"

He turned to look at me, his face untroubled. "To kill myself. I saw Sid lying on the floor and suddenly I didn't want to go on living. It just didn't seem worth it anymore." He frowned, trying to keep the memory straight. "But when I got to the den, I got confused about things. So, I lay down on the bed to think." He shrugged. "And the next thing I know it's morning and your mom's asleep beside me and Pepper's nudging me and whining because he wants to go out. So I got up and let him out." He hesitated. "Next I think your mom and that Marston guy took me to the hospital. I don't quite remember."

I took a breath. "But you weren't going to hurt us then? That wasn't why you went for the shotgun?"

"No, I'd never hurt you."

I had to ask, had to find out once and for all. "Then you still love us, don't you? You still love me?"

For a second, his face worked as if deep inside he was trying to find something again. But he couldn't and the expression faded, leaving his face calm. "I've tried, Shar. I tried very hard at first. When I came home from the hospital that first time, I stared and stared at you, trying to remember what I'd felt before. But it wouldn't come, Shar. It just never came back again."

We stared into each other's eyes for a long moment. "I'm sorry, Dad," I said.

He nodded. "Yes, I think I am too. Or I'd like to be. It's hard to know sometimes."

Pepper was feeling ignored and nudged Dad's arm. Dad started slowing stroking Pepper's glossy coat, his gaze wandering off across the smooth water of the lake. Then suddenly he stiffened.

"What is it, Dad?"

"Geese." He stood and peered at the northern sky. And sure enough, there they were, a great chevron of geese against the clear blue, their honking like laughter as they flew high and fast toward the south.

I stroll home from the lake across the fields at the edge of town. Dad is there walking beside me, while Pepper roves back and forth hunting for mice. I remember the dad I lost and I miss him. And, I'll give this stranger what love I can in memory of that dad I once had. But I'm not going to feel sorry for him anymore, because maybe what he's got isn't so bad. He and Pepper are a lot alike. They don't get into complicated stuff; they just enjoy eating and playing with a ball and feeling the sunshine. They've got Mom, Alex, Sid, and me to worry about all the other things. But we can handle it. Maybe we'll have to do it for years—or maybe not so long. I don't know. But I do know that the stars are coming out on a cool autumn evening and that there's a Halloween dance at school. I'm going to dress up and join all those other people in costumes and masks. And, you know something? I'm going to have fun. You bet.